A
THEORY
OF
HAUNTING

Other books in the Satellites series

A
THEORY
OF
HAUNTING

SARAH MONETTE

Sarah Monette

SOLARIS

First published 2023 by Solaris
an imprint of Rebellion Publishing Ltd,
Riverside House, Osney Mead,
Oxford, OX2 0ES, UK

www.solarisbooks.com

ISBN: 978-1-83786-110-1

Copyright © 2023 Sarah Monette

Designed & typeset by Rebellion Publishing

To Shirley Jackson (1916-1965),
the master of the haunted house story

THE CURRENT OWNER of *Thirdhop Scarp* claims that the name is a contraction of "third hope," but this idea is etymologically dubious in the extreme; still improbable but far more likely is the local explanation: that if you fall off the escarpment, you reach the bottom in three hops. Tragedy and scandal have surrounded the house for eighty years, since it was built by the occultist Zenobia Webster Tull, and given the choice, I would have preferred to have nothing to do with it.

However.

I

ONE TUESDAY AFTERNOON, Dr Starkweather, the director of the Samuel Mather Parrington Museum, called me to his office, where he bade me sit and then unnerved me horribly by staring at me, frowning, turning a pen over and over in his thick fingers. Finally, he made a curious sound, half sigh, half snort, and said, "I have just returned from Byzantium."

"Er," I said. Byzantium was the name of the Parrington mansion, where Samuel Mather Parrington's daughters, widowed Blanche and spinster Griselda, still lived; its appearance in Dr Starkweather's conversation was never a propitious omen.

Dr Starkweather's baleful glare moved from me to the portrait of Samuel Mather Parrington that dominated his office. "It seems that Miss Parrington has become involved with the circle of Marcus Oleander."

"Oh dear."

"Precisely, Mr Booth," said Dr Starkweather.

Marcus Oleander (for such was the name under which

he presented himself) had been in the newspapers rather a lot in the last few years; he had purchased the house at Thirdhop Scarp, announcing it to have been the dying wish of his mentor, T. Zacharias Tull, that he, Oleander, inherit the house and the Tull legacy. He had started an esoteric order called the Order Aurorae Aeternae, which seemed to be mostly a society club for dilettantes in the occult, but was definitely a means for Marcus Oleander to promote his own learning, wisdom, and alleged occult power. He was always willing to say something outrageous to newspaper men if it meant he would get in the newspapers.

"Mrs Crowe is not pleased," Dr Starkweather said grimly. "She believes that Marcus Oleander is nothing more than a confidence man. She wishes the museum to investigate Mr Oleander's occult claims, and she would prefer that we find evidence of charlatanry that she can present to her sister to persuade her to drop the connection."

Convincing the eternally credulous Griselda Parrington that Marcus Oleander was not what he said he was sounded a little like trying to level a mountain with nothing more than a spoon.

"But how can the museum possibly...?"

"Mrs Crowe understands from her sister that Oleander is in need of someone to catalogue his library. I said you would be happy to oblige."

Nothing could have been farther from the truth. I hate travel, hate meeting strangers, and am most dreadfully bad at any kind of social interaction. I yelped and scrambled for defense: "I, er... that is, Dr Starkweather, I... I don't..."

"Mrs Crowe asked for you," Dr Starkweather said even more grimly, "specifically."

While it was Griselda Parrington who interested herself most keenly in the business of the museum, it was Blanche Parrington Crowe who controlled the Parrington estate. And the Parrington estate was still, nearly thirty years after Samuel Mather Parrington's death, the museum's principal benefactor. I have worked as an archivist at the Parrington Museum for fifteen years, specializing in books on the occult and other arcane subjects. My job has brought me into contact with the supernatural far more often than I would like, but it is my only passion, and I cannot give it up.

"...When is Mr Oleander expecting me?"

Short of tendering my resignation on the spot, there was nothing else I could say.

THE LAST OWNER of Thirdhop Scarp, before Marcus Oleander, had been John Aloysius Cathcart, and on the train trip from the city to the nearest station to Thirdhop Scarp, in Pittmanville, I considered his sanguinary history.

I had not known him personally, but he had been an acquaintance of my guardian's, stigmatized as parvenu and pushing, but a valuable business associate nevertheless. He had bought Thirdhop Scarp when T. Zacharias Tull had died, intestate and—as it transpired—massively in debt. In the last years of my adolescence, I had listened to unending speculation about what had happened to the famous Tull fortune and how T. Zacharias could possibly have squandered it all. J. A. Cathcart was regarded with a mixture of revulsion and grudging approbation for having taken advantage of the situation with such promptness and vigor. People made uneasy jokes about the ghost of T. Zacharias expressing *his* opinion, but nothing of the sort happened. Even Mrs Cathcart, who had reportedly been very nervous about the house, admitted that there was nothing wrong with it at all.

Until there was.

But by the time anyone knew, it was already far too late.

Just past midnight on the eighth of August, the year I turned seventeen, the servants at Thirdhop Scarp were woken by screams—terrible screams, their testimony at the trial agreed, a woman's voice screaming in terror and mortal agony and under that, a roaring noise, more like an animal than anything human. That roaring continued after the screams could no longer be heard, continued for at least half an hour, and when it finally stopped, it was nearly half an hour more before the terrified housekeeper and equally terrified gardener climbed the stairs to the nursery and found J. A. Cathcart cupping his eldest daughter's heart in his hands as tenderly as he would a wounded bird.

The prosecution reconstructed the crime for the jury, with floor plans and photographs and an inexorable attention to detail, and I read it all compulsively in the newspapers. Mr Cathcart had started with his wife—the experts disagreed about whether she had been awake or asleep when the first blow fell, but she had still been alive, and screaming, when his tenth blow severed the major vessels in her neck and very nearly decapitated her. She was dead when he dismembered her and tucked her butchered body carefully into bed.

Then he went up to the nursery. Laura Dunaphy, the children's nurse, tried to stop him and was smashed aside. The prosecution submitted as evidence Laura Dunaphy's nightdress with the bloody print of a man's bare foot on the shoulder, where Mr Cathcart had braced himself to yank the hatchet out of her head.

(Amazingly, the blow did not kill her immediately. At some point after Mr Cathcart left her, she staggered to her feet, down two flights of stairs, leaving bloody handprints on the wall with every step, and out the front door, where she collapsed and died in the driveway.)

The youngest Cathcart daughter, Louisa, had the room closest to the stairs; he started there and worked his way back: Louisa, then Constance, then across the hall to John Aloysius, Jr., where he lingered, hacking his son's body into unidentifiable meat, and then to his eldest daughter Rose's room, where he was found.

No one knew what had caused the roaring noise, a fact which made both prosecution and defense very uneasy. It was of no earthly use to ask J. A. Cathcart, because as far as he was concerned, he had had no part in his family's deaths at all. At his trial, and for the rest of his life, John Aloysius Cathcart insisted he was innocent. No one believed him.

At the trial, no one even believed that *he* believed his own story (that he had woken in bed next to his wife's dead body and raced upstairs only to find his children murdered as well), but after the trial, after his conviction, he deluged the world with letters insisting that the evidence had been faked, the witnesses suborned, that someone had gotten away with the murder of two women and four children. As the years passed, his theories became wilder and wilder; by the time he died, he was insisting that his wife was not dead, that the body in the bed had been someone else, that Helen Redding

Cathcart was hiding, in fear for her life, in the attic of Thirdhop Scarp. He died begging the prison doctor to find her and protect her, and so convincing was his belief that the doctor actually organized a search party.

They found nothing.

I WAS MET at the train station in Pittmanville by a silent, broad-shouldered colored man in a chauffeur's uniform. The only time we spoke on the way to Thirdhop Scarp was when he sneezed. I said, "God bless you," and he said, "Thank you."

We drove endlessly through the peaceful, bucolic countryside, then turned and drove up an equally endless driveway through a dark and tangled forest, as if we were driving into a story from the Brothers Grimm, finally coming out where the driveway made a circle in front of Thirdhop Scarp.

The house was in the Gothic Revival style and had a tall central building with two relatively stubby wings and an addition to the end of the south wing that, while in the same style, did not entirely assimilate with the house as a whole. To the right of the front doors was an enormous bay window, and I found it distressing that there was not an answering bay window to the left, when the house was otherwise perfectly symmetrical.

Marcus Oleander was waiting on the front steps—tall, as lean as Shakespeare's Cassius, with pale blond hair and gleaming, glinting eyes—and greeted me, waving away the butler, with such relentless cordiality as to make me extremely nervous. He insisted on giving me a tour of the main house, including Zenobia Webster Tull's combination study and parlor, with its massive bay window and delicate ivy trellis wallpaper; Oleander assured me it had been restored to match contemporary descriptions and every photograph he could find. One of the photographs hung in an ornate frame over her desk, showing a stout, fashionable, white-haired lady with a malignant eye. Oleander clearly enjoyed playing tour guide—showing off his expensive toys to a less fortunate child—and for a while I despaired of ever being freed from his hospitality. But when he finally led me down the hall through the south wing to the library, he explained the situation clearly enough.

The case was that Marcus Oleander had recently inherited the libraries of two English friends of his and had had them shipped from London to Thirdhop Scarp. Both gentlemen had been fanatical but hopelessly chaotic bibliophiles of an esoteric bent; neither collection had a full catalogue, and the problem was exacerbated by both the library of T. Zacharias Tull, which Mr Oleander had acquired with Thirdhop Scarp, and by his own library, the catalogue of which (he said with another expansive, gleaming smile) was several years out of date. "I'm afraid I'm much better at the collecting than the cataloguing, Mr Booth."

"Most, er, people are."

He laughed as if I had said something amusing. "I'm sure that's true. In any event, while I know there must be redundant volumes, I have no idea how to go about finding them or…" He trailed off and shrugged in a way that I was perhaps meant to find charming.

"I understand," I said hastily, before he felt it necessary to charm me further. "You, er, you realize… that is, this may be a very lengthy process."

"I should think so," he said, laughing again. "I

appreciate you surrendering your long weekend like this, and I was hoping you might be willing to do so again, from time to time, until the job is done. You will not find Thirdhop Scarp's hospitality stingy or begrudging."

"I... er, I'm sure I..."

"Splendid!" said Mr Oleander, as if the matter were settled. "And here's the library." He opened a door onto an oddly shaped, glassed-in porch and laughed at my expression. "Originally, the library was entirely separate from the main house, but as Mr Tull got older, he got more particular—first a roof, then screens, and finally the glass. *Here's* the library." He pushed open a set of beautifully carved double doors and waved me through.

The library, which T. Zacharias Tull had added to the house after his mother's death, was a long room, no doubt deliberately reminiscent of a cathedral nave. The tall narrow windows that marked each of the seven aisles were stained glass, uninspired but attractive. Wall sconces flanked each window, refitted clumsily for electricity. Even when Oleander turned them on, the room remained dim and thick with shadows. There were books everywhere: on shelves, on the floor, still in crates with the lids pried off like clamshells. The three partial catalogues were on the table in front of the doors, along with a pile of bound ledgers and several stacks of index cards.

"I can see you are panting to get to your work," Mr Oleander said behind me, making me jump. I had forgotten he was there. "I shan't detain you any longer. There's a bell pull by the door. Ring if you need anything, and feel free to wander the house and grounds. We dine at eight." With that, he sauntered out, pulling the doors closed behind him.

I spent the rest of the afternoon in a preliminary survey of the terrain, as it were, reading the shelves and digging through the open crates. Most of what I found on the shelves was unremarkable: histories (including Gibbon, Macaulay, and Bourke), biographies (including Aubrey and Boswell), eighteenth century novels, Elizabethan plays, the complete works of Mrs Gaskell. I spotted a few items that looked promising though. Oettinger, Makropoulos, a very battered copy of Bevington's *Bestiary*. And the books in the crates were more promising still. There were another three crates along the wall to the right of the doors, but I needed a crowbar to open them.

At quarter to seven I took myself off to walk in the grounds for half an hour before going to dress for dinner. A period of quiet reflection, while it would not make the ordeal of dining with Marcus Oleander any less dreadful, might give me strength to withstand it. I walked as far as the ornamental lake to the northeast of the house. Although in general I admire and enjoy the use of water in landscaping, I had to admit that this particular execution of the idea had perhaps been a mistake. The lake—for it was just slightly too large to call a pond—seemed curiously swollen, turbid and much too still. The smell of stagnation and decay was as heavy as a pall, and there was nothing, not a noise, not a motion, to suggest that anything lived here, but at the same time, there was an oppressive feeling—not just of being watched, but almost of being *stalked,* as if I were perhaps only a single wrong step away from being caught by something both cruel and hungry. I did not linger, returning to the better maintained and more pleasant parts of the garden.

I was walking through the formal elegance of the rose garden, pleasing even though nothing was in bloom, when a voice said, "You're the librarian, aren't you?"

I turned, and the speaker emerged from the shadow of a trellised arbor. He was a boy, sixteen or seventeen at most, tall, coltish, but not as gawky as I had been at his age—as I still was. Under straight, rather heavy eyebrows, his eyes were brilliant and dark as night. His voice was deep, although I guessed only recently broken, and his elocution had the excellence of careful training.

I said, "I am an archivist, yes."

"Is there a difference?"

I explained, and when I had done, as if I had passed some sort of test, he extended his hand. "Alexis Rigby."

I shook his hand quickly and reluctantly. "Kyle Murchison Booth."

"Charmed," he said.

I turned away from his brilliant stare and said rather desperately, "Are you a member of Mr Oleander's, er...?"

"What, the O.A.A.? No, I thank you. They're a little ridiculous, don't you think, prancing about in their mystic bed sheets?"

The Order Aurorae Aeternae favored the Greek in their ceremonial garb. This information, too, had been in the newspapers because Marcus Oleander made sure everything was; I recalled some very unflattering photographs. "You, er, sound like a skeptic," I said— even a youth would be a welcome ally.

"No," he said, and his smile shocked me, for it was both sly and terribly weary, "I wouldn't say that."

He wanted me to ask; I was uncertain whether I wished to oblige him, having learned long ago that once one agreed, even tacitly, even unwittingly, to that sort of game, one was as hopelessly ensnared as a foolish thrashing fly in a spider's web.

Before I found a reply that would be both polite and noncommittal, the brazen voice of a gong spoke across the garden.

"Half an hour 'til dinner," said Alexis Rigby. "You'd best go change clothes."

"Yes," I said, and I fled from him in long strides across the dusk-drowned garden to the house.

I DO NOT like Spiritualism. Its practitioners are mostly frauds; those who are sincere are frequently also lamentably misguided, children playing with knives and matches. There are exceptions, but the unscrupulous and the naïve are far more common, and the nature of my work is such that I encounter them far more often than I would wish to.

Marcus Oleander oozed fraud from every golden scale; most of those at his dinner table that evening were gulls, as the Elizabethans would have called them, entering into their own fleecing with self-important enthusiasm. Counting myself, there were twelve, with our host an oppressively jovial thirteenth. Conversation in the early part of the meal was devoted to slandering an absent fourteenth. Mr Paul Merridew had sent a telegram saying he was unavoidably detained, but the consensus at the table was that he had, in the bluff military language of Captain Theodore Blackburn, "funked it."

Captain Blackburn and his wife Myra were the guardians of Alexis Rigby. They were not members of the Order, and they were not gulls. I suspected strongly that they were charlatans every bit as adroit as Marcus

Oleander. They certainly knew how to gild the lily they had in Alexis Rigby, who I gathered was a medium already attracting a great deal of attention in occult circles. It was, or at least Myra Blackburn made it sound as if it were, something of a coup for Mr Oleander to have gotten him to Thirdhop Scarp, and the Order fawned accordingly. Alexis himself remained exquisitely polite, although he did not quite bother to hide how tedious he found it all. He seemed a different person from the one I had met in the garden: smoother, stiller, darker. Too much like the ornamental lake, I thought, watching Alexis listen indifferently as Mr Oleander flattered him, and controlled a shiver. It was not a happy thought.

I noticed that Mr Oleander was the cynosure of all feminine eyes, except possibly the calculating ones of Myra Blackburn. Miss Parrington—who had greeted me brightly and then forgotten about me—was by no means the worst, and my neck and ears burned with vicarious mortification. It was cruel of Mr Oleander to encourage them, but I saw no recognition of that cruelty in the married men around the table. The other unmarried man, Michael Kitchener, was Mr Oleander's lieutenant, stocky and dark, with a sharp widow's peak and an equally sharp smile. He was prominent in the assassination of Paul Merridew's character, and it was he, having become bored with this pastime, who said over the roast pork with apples and chestnuts, "Well, really, it isn't as if all is lost. What about you, Mr Booth?"

He caught me utterly unprepared. I said, "Er," choked, and sought refuge in my water glass.

Mr Oleander said, "Michael, that's not fair. I'm sure Mr Booth has no interest in our foolish little forays after knowledge."

As a tactical move, it was perhaps a little blatant for Machiavelli—but then again, perhaps not. It was unquestionably effective, for everyone instantly focused on me like hunting dogs given a scent. I shrank back from the evangelical light in the women's eyes and said hastily, "I have no opinion."

"Oh, but you should, Mr Booth," Mr Oleander said; I looked up just in time to catch his smirk. "You should join us for the séance tomorrow evening."

"No," I said, far more sharply than I intended, and therefore added placatingly, "Thank you."

"You shouldn't reject something you have no knowledge of," Mrs Hallett said. "I should think a librarian would understand the importance of being open-minded."

"Mr Booth informs me that the correct term is 'archivist'," Alexis Rigby said, smooth and dark, twisting information shared into pedantry, twisting understanding into mockery. The company followed his lead like sheep after a bellwether. I was unsurprised. I held mulishly, miserably, to my refusal, and escaped as soon as I could.

I had brought with me my favorite collection of Clémence Renard's poetry, *Les Yeux d'Anne Boleyn*, and once I had performed my evening ablutions, I settled in to read. I had no expectation of sleeping, and I was certainly wide awake when I finished "*Les prières de la pluie*." But I remember being in the middle of "*Le roi des places sombres*," just as the mad narrator cries, "*Seulement moi, c'est le champion des ombres!*" and then I was somewhere else.

I was trapped in a windowless, doorless, airless room. It was black and suffocating; the walls were smooth unyielding plaster. I shouted, then screamed, and pounded on the walls until my hands were slick with blood and I was choking for breath, but no one came. I knew—the way one does know things in dreams— that there were people nearby, but they did not hear me. Worse, as the night wore on, I knew that even if they heard me, they did not care. I was trapped there all night, unable to free myself until the merciful sunlight across my closed eyes dazzled me awake.

I did not expect the Order Aurorae Aeternae to be early risers, and they were not. My only company at the breakfast table was Miss Parrington. She was all twigs and cobwebs and the mindless chatter of a windchime. It was restful, though, because she did not expect me to answer her; tremendous self-absorption can sometimes be almost the same as tact. She told me a great deal about her own occult experiences, and asked not a single question about mine.

I was grateful to escape without meeting anyone else, and it was with difficulty that I resisted the impulse to lock the doors of the library behind me. I was left in peace all morning, making steady if glacial progress on the task of writing catalogue cards for each of the books physically present in the library. The hopeful delusions of the catalogues could wait.

I emerged dust-streaked and ink-blotched for lunch, and the Order Aurorae Aeternae and their guests eyed me with sidelong amusement. Since the table was deeply involved in a discussion of the correct rules under which to play croquet, I was spared conversational gambits; I only wished I could have brought my work with me. I was opening the doors to the library, already and gratefully planning my afternoon's tasks, when Alexis Rigby called my name.

I closed the doors without entering and turned to face him. "Aren't you, er, playing croquet?"

"Oh, in a moment. Will you come to the séance tonight?"

"I don't know. The occult doesn't... that is, it is not a subject that holds much interest for me."

"No?" he said, as if he saw falsehood plainly on my face.

"Not as you understand it, no."

His eyebrows went up. "I beg your pardon. I didn't mean to hit a nerve."

Oh, of course you did, I thought. I did not say it. After a moment, he continued lightly, "And in any event, please don't tar me with the O.A.A.'s brush. Their drivel certainly isn't what I understand as the occult, either."

The way he spoke—so much as one adult expert to another—worried me. "How long have you been a medium?"

"All my life," he said with a dazzlingly sunny smile.

"I meant how long have you been, er, giving séances?"

"Since I was thirteen or so."

"And your guardians don't object?"

"Myra's my teacher."

"Ah," I said, now even more worried. But we heard Myra Blackburn's voice calling, "Alexis! Darling, where have you wandered off to?" and Alexis said, "Whoops. Duty calls."

He strode away, strong and arrogant as a young god, and I, dusty, shabby, no longer young even if I ever had been, returned to the library.

THE CATALOGUING PROCEEDED sedately; the only progress I made on my true task at Thirdhop Scarp was the discovery of a copy of Isaiah Hope Turnbull's forgery of the *Book of Whispers*, one of the few books among Mr Oleander's personal collection that showed signs of having been read. Read and used, for the marginalia made it plain that the teachings of the Order Aurorae Aeternae had been cribbed from the engaging, inventive, and completely untrustworthy Mr Turnbull. To anyone with any knowledge of the occult, this was the proof of charlatanry I had been ordered to find, and for a giddy moment, I thought I might be free of Thirdhop Scarp by Monday morning.

Reality reasserted its iron grip almost immediately. The person who had to be persuaded was not, in fact, someone with any knowledge of the occult. Nor—as I considered my experience of Miss Parrington's "finds" for the museum with growing dismay—was she someone with any meaningful grasp of the concept that one source of information might be more trustworthy than another. Miss Parrington, as far as I had ever been able to tell, believed *everything*—everything she read, everything she was told, everything she heard via fourth or fifth hand gossip—and persuading someone that universally credulous that she ought *not* to believe a particular person because he had cribbed his wisdom from a well-known fake... I had heard my colleagues have this discussion with Miss Parrington innumerable times; I had even, once, attempted it myself and been shamefully routed by her confident and extensive list of all the things—from dowsing to past lives to the lost continent of Atlantis— that had been sneered at as frauds but were now known to be true. She had even sternly quoted *Hamlet* at me, and I had conceded defeat.

Thus, my proof was useless, no matter how damning. It was probably resentment that made me reckless, made me say at dinner in answer to Michael Kitchener's delicately barbed question about my day's work, "I found a very nice copy of the 1888 forgery of the *Book of Whispers*."

It was petty and childish of me to be gratified by the furor I caused.

They did not believe me. I was not surprised. What was a little startling was the vehemence with which Marcus Oleander defended the book. I realized, of course, that he was trying to maintain the belief of his flock and at the same time impress the Blackburns, but his fervor was still remarkable and not at all what I had come to expect from him.

"It's all very well to sneer at it as a fake," he said, "but that's just because you haven't seen the wisdom of its teachings." Miss Parrington and Mrs Hallett were nodding eagerly. "When you come to the séance tonight, you'll—"

"Actually," I said, "I would, er, prefer not to."

The company was quick to inundate me with reproaches and persuasions. There was, though, a single stunned moment before any of them could muster a response, and that moment—that and Alexis Rigby's smothered choke of laughter—gave me unwonted strength, and I stood my ground.

I did not attend the séance that evening in Thirdhop Scarp.

Instead, I returned to the library. This time, I did lock the doors behind me, and felt immeasurably better for having done so. I worked steadily and peacefully for several hours; midnight came and went, and it was only very slowly that I became aware that I was listening for something. For a voice. A child's voice. *What on earth?*

I thought, for Thirdhop Scarp was hardly the sort of house to welcome children, and even if there had been children here, I was alone in the library with the doors locked. There was no reason I should expect to hear a child... a child singing. Yet I could not stop listening for it, the way one listens for footsteps in one's home after midnight.

And it was not that I had *heard* a child; I was perfectly sure I had not. It was that I was listening, more and more of my attention focused on hearing something—a child's voice, a French folksong—that every instinct insisted was going to become audible... *now*.

But it did not.

And did not and did not, until my temples throbbed from the strain of listening for something that simply was not there. Finally, unable to continue working, I skulked cautiously up to my bedroom. No one else was abroad, and I wondered if they were all virtuously in bed or if they still sat in a circle, surrounded by candlelight, listening to Alexis Rigby tell them lies.

I dozed, barely, on and off the rest of the night, still half listening for a child's voice.

SUNDAY MORNING, THE public rooms of Thirdhop Scarp were desolate; even Miss Parrington was not abroad. I breakfasted alone. I locked myself in the library again and deliberately skipped lunch. Hunger seemed a small price to pay for avoiding another encounter with the Order Aurorae Aeternae.

I left Thirdhop Scarp that afternoon, and only wished I could believe I would never have to return. Marcus Oleander emerged from his lair and saw me off amidst a profusion of insincere apologies for having made me "uncomfortable" at dinner the night before. I went red, flinched from his handshake, and mumbled something unintelligible even to myself. Fortunately, at that moment Mrs Hallett's penetrating voice was raised in a summons from inside the house; I shamelessly took advantage of the opportunity, grabbing my valise and all but diving into the waiting automobile.

The chauffeur neither objected nor questioned; he simply put the vehicle in gear and started for the train station. I spent the train trip back to town rehearsing my arguments as to why Dr Starkweather should not make me return to Thirdhop Scarp. They were excellent arguments, well-reasoned and persuasive, and on Monday, Dr Starkweather did not give me a chance to utter a word of them. He had come into his office late that morning to be greeted by a summons to Byzantium, and when he returned, blackly furious, it was to issue a ukase: I was to spend every weekend at Thirdhop Scarp from now until Doomsday, unless and until I could pry Griselda Parrington away from Marcus Oleander's influence. Apparently, she had telegraphed to her sister to tell her she had, at long last, spoken to a real ghost.

II

My second weekend at Thirdhop Scarp passed much as the first, save that this time, no one bothered with trying to talk to me. They were all much too busy, and I was glad of it. There was an almost electrical atmosphere in the house, a constant sense of people conferring in whispers and rushing to and fro on important errands. There were also nearly double the number of guests. If it was not the entire roster of the Order Aurorae Aeternae it was surely very close. I noticed in particular the delinquent Mr Merridew, a young man with the sharp-angled face of a predator who seemed to consider himself Mr Kitchener's rival. His conversation was entirely comprised of implication and disdain, and all too many of his fellow guests appeared willing to follow his lead.

I spent as much time in the library as I could. When my hand cramped from writing, I took to exploring the shelves and boxes, deliberately searching out the most neglected corners of the room, things that Marcus Oleander might not have found yet—or might not have thought to remove.

My motivation was nothing more than pettiness, a child's desire to have a secret from a bully, something to hug to myself as I sat, *persona non grata*, among the scurrilous whispers of the Order Aurorae Aeternae, and I did not truly expect to find anything more interesting than the already-discovered Turnbull forgery. But the hunt was itself a pleasure, and I pursued it with a certain amount of rigor—which was how, very late Saturday afternoon, I came across a secret after all.

A shorter man might not have found it, for only a man as tall as myself, or a very thorough housekeeper, would have noticed the thin manila envelope lying on top of the grandfather clock to the left of the doors. Between its natural color and the thick layer of dust, it was nearly invisible. I picked it up, sneezed twice, and took it back to the table. I opened it carefully. A stack of paper, high quality, maybe twenty sheets. The top page said, in copybook perfect cursive, *A History of the Webster and Tull Families, with remarks upon their principal residence at Thirdhop Scarp, by A. C. Tull.*

Amateur genealogy, then. I thumbed quickly through the pages, noting a family tree that looked like a child of the Hydra, and then returned to my proper work. But, feeling ridiculously and exhilaratingly guilty, I smuggled the envelope and its contents upstairs with me when I went to clean up before dinner.

That evening, there was no séance. Mr Oleander announced at dinner that Alexis had a sick headache; Myra Blackburn assured everyone with a charming smile that he was prone to them and it was nothing to worry about. "He'll be fine tomorrow," she said, "and perhaps we can have an afternoon séance—sometimes they work surprisingly well with the more fragile spirits."

The Order Aurorae Aeternae grumbled as sulkily as children denied a trip to the zoo, but allowed themselves to be mollified. Borne up by the knowledge that I would be safely on a train by the time this séance did or did not take place, I endured the rest of dinner, and the attendant and singularly witless conversation, and escaped the company as soon as I could, retreating to my room and the *History of the Webster and Tull Families*.

It transpired immediately that A. C. Tull was Agnes Christabel Tull, youngest daughter of Zenobia Webster Tull, and I turned back to that hydra-like genealogy I had noticed earlier. Mrs Tull had had six children: T. Zacharias (whose given name turned out to be Terence), Emily, Cecilia, Randolph, Violet, and Agnes. Agnes's interest in genealogy and family history, she wrote, came from her father, Leonard Tull, who had been an amateur historian, particularly interested in Pittmanville and the brooding cliff of Thirdhop Scarp itself. When Leonard Tull died, he left his papers to Agnes, and in sorting through them, she had discovered some things that she thought were important enough to write down.

In large part, I disagreed with her. The early history of the Websters and Tulls in America was undistinguished (Tulls) or a mass of unsubstantiated speculations (Websters) that made me think very poorly of Leonard Tull's merit as a historian; the history of Thirdhop Scarp seemed to be a chronicle of subsistence farming, with the inevitable attendant deaths and epidemics, until Zenobia Webster Tull, newly married, newly a mother, and newly acclaimed as a Spiritualist, returned in triumph to her hometown and began building a house which was to be "larger, more beautiful, and in every way more grand" than anything that had ever been there before.

The history of the building of Thirdhop Scarp, however, was possibly of greater interest than Agnes Tull had realized. Zenobia Webster Tull had hired the region's brightest young architectural star, Phythias Ormont, to design her mansion, and she had spent money lavishly in an effort to speed the process. Moreover, she had had an unusually close partnership with Ormont, not only visiting his offices frequently, but bringing him out to Thirdhop Scarp. Her husband remained in New York until construction was complete, becoming a railroad baron in a quiet way and providing the money for her absurdly ostentatious house.

But the thing that accelerated my pulse was Leonard Tull's account, transmitted through Agnes, of Phythias Ormont's death. I had not known there *were* any accounts of Phythias Ormont's death; his family had hushed the matter up so obsessively that the only places one might find him mentioned nowadays were architectural histories of the region and Pentecost Ormont's first collection of poetry, *Kind Vampires*, which included a poem entitled, "Of Whom We Do Not Speak." I had not even known that he had died at Thirdhop Scarp. But Leonard Tull described (in his daughter's perfect, characterless copperplate) hearing the gunshot and finding Ormont, still gripping the pistol so tightly that his fingers could not be pried off it, and with half his brain spattered across Zenobia Webster Tull's expensive Italian wallpaper.

The *History* ended very abruptly mid-sentence at the bottom of the twenty-third page. I wondered whether Agnes had been distracted from making a fair copy or whether the rest of the manuscript had been lost. At this remove, either explanation was plausible. I put the papers very carefully back in their envelope and crept as cautiously as a burglar back down to the library to replace them where I had found them. I hated to do it, so much so that I found it difficult to stop fidgeting with the envelope, but they were self-evidently safe where they were, and I could not construct a scenario for getting them out of the house that would be successful. Marcus Oleander would certainly appropriate them as his own the instant he learned of their existence—and no doubt enshrine them in his recreation of Zenobia Webster Tull's study—and if I stole them… theft is frequently tempting to archivists and curators, but it invariably causes more problems than it solves. In this case, I would merely be trading one impenetrable obscurity for another; they could not be published without their provenance, and Dr Starkweather would have my head on a platter if I caused Oleander to bring suit against the Parrington. And rightly so.

Since I had reached the library unnoticed, I decided it might be wiser to stay for a while rather than risk the return trip immediately: I had heard voices from the drawing room and seen the long block of lamplight from the partially open door. I would wait until the company had gone to bed before returning to my room. It was not as if I did not have work I could be doing.

All things have the defects of their virtues; in my case, my ability to concentrate meant that it was nearly four hours before I raised my head again—two in the morning. I felt immediately guilty, although there was no reason to: a dreary hangover from my childhood and adolescence. My guardian had seemed to feel that no one would willingly be awake past midnight unless they had nefarious and possibly even diabolical purposes. My protests that I was simply not sleepy were never believed, and in fact caused him to regard me with more suspicion than ever.

I did need rest; aware of myself again, I could feel my eyes burning with fatigue, and there were knots of pain in my shoulders. I was in the act of pushing my chair back when the conviction hit me, hard and brutal and breath-wrenching: there was something waiting for me on the other side of the library doors.

The hairs stood slowly on the back of my neck.

I could feel it, greedy and patient, and more than that, I could smell it, a damp, stale odor, completely unlike the musty scent of books. The smell of the ornamental lake, I realized, and my hands cramped shut in a shudder. When I listened, holding my breath, I could hear a snuffling sound, and the muffled, squelching, scratchy noise of something pawing at the door, as if it was trying to grasp the doorknob and failing.

Thank God I locked the doors, I thought, and dragged in a noisy, necessary breath, sinking slowly back into my chair. I had no inclination to convince myself I was imagining things, even less inclination to test the hypothesis by opening the door. I considered for a mad moment going out the window, but just as quickly discarded the notion, for at least in here I had the library doors to protect me. I was trapped, and if I sat here listening to those soft frustrated noises, I would go mad in truth.

I picked up my pen and a fresh index card, and went back to work.

As THE DARK began to soften grayly toward dawn, the thing in the hallway heaved a tremendous wet, snuffling sigh and shuffled away. I waited until the sun was fully up before I went anywhere near the doors.

There was nothing there, of course, and no sign that there ever had been, except for what might have been a slight tackiness around the doorknob—or might merely have been my imagination.

I LEFT THIRDHOP Scarp as soon as I could on Sunday. Marcus Oleander saw me off again, as loudly regretful as if I were his oldest and most treasured friend. But before I had to come up with any intelligible reply, Alexis Rigby appeared, and Marcus Oleander forgot that I existed.

I did not blame him for being solicitous; Alexis looked dreadful, the color and vitality seeming to have been leached out of him, the darkness of his eyes now shadowed, lusterless. I remembered wondering the night before if the sick headache had been merely a convenient excuse, but clearly that had been unjust. I thought perhaps Alexis had wanted to say something to me, but he did not get the chance; Mr Oleander hustled him back inside, scolding him for over-exerting himself. I hesitated a moment, wondering if I should go after them, but the truth was that I did not want to. "Am I my brother's keeper?" I muttered as I got into the waiting automobile, feeling guilty again and annoyed at my own guilt.

"Pardon, sir?" said the chauffeur, polite but utterly uninterested, and I would have thanked him for it if I could have explained what I meant without sounding like a madman.

"…Nothing," I said. "Please, let's go."

"Yes, sir." The automobile started for the train station; I had no sense of relief or freedom, already dreading my return on Friday.

"Do you lock your door at night?" I said suddenly.

"Beg pardon, sir?"

"Do you? Lock your door?"

He turned his head just far enough to give me an uneasy flick of a glance, but said, "Yes, sir." And added, "All the staff do."

"Good," I said.

Neither of us said anything more until we reached the train station. I got out, my valise banging awkwardly against my legs, and just before I shut the door, he said, only loud enough that I heard him, "There are stories about Thirdhop Scarp."

III

ON THE WEDNESDAY, as I was sorting through the contents of a box one of the junior curators had found in the coat check of the now disused North Lobby, someone knocked on the door.

"Come in, Mr Lucent," I said wearily. It would be his fifth visit today, and it was barely past noon.

But it was not Mr Lucent.

Alexis Rigby, perfect as a fashion plate, closed the door carefully behind him and said, "Have I caught you at a bad time?"

"What on earth are you—er, that is to say... er, hello."

"Hello," he answered demurely, his amusement politely concealed. "May I speak to you for a moment?"

"...Of course."

"I wondered if you might be willing to help me with something."

I had learned, at great cost, to be wary of doing favors. "What sort of, er, help?"

"May I... is there somewhere I can sit?"

It was not an unreasonable question. Every chair in the office, save the one behind my desk, was covered with papers and plaster casts, envelopes with foreign stamps, daguerreotypes protected against the light with cloth and cardboard, woodcuts barbarically sundered from long-perished books. I said, "Er."

"Oh, never mind." He turned away abruptly and began to pace. "He's a fraud, you know."

"Who is?"

The words poured out: "Marcus Oleander—if that's his real name, which God knows I doubt. He didn't inherit those books you're cataloguing. He bought them at auction. In bulk. And he didn't know T. Zacharias Tull, either. He's a fraud, and he *hates* it. It's why he invited us."

"I'm sorry, I don't—"

"He wants Myra to teach him." Alexis stopped pacing; his tone had lightened into amusement. "Well, he *thought* he wanted the captain to teach him, but Myra soon set him straight."

"But to teach him what?"

"Well, Myra calls it necromancy, but Tull called it something else. He was Myra's teacher, you know." Horrifyingly, he giggled. "Oleander doesn't know that yet. Myra's not ready to spring it on him."

"So she's teaching him necromancy?" Dear God, such a terrible idea. More than ever, I wanted nothing to do with Thirdhop Scarp.

"You could say that." Alexis moved his shoulders as if he was trying to shrug something off. "And they... they did something."

"Something?" I said.

"Friday night. It gave me the worst headache I've ever

had. Myra says it's all part of Tull's teachings, but this was... this was different."

"Different from what?"

"From a proper séance," Alexis said. "The séances we did before were fine. Plenty of activity for the punters—sorry, the O.A.A. Two girls and a little boy, and an even littler girl."

"The Cathcarts," I said, thinking of the child I had never quite heard singing in the library. "They were murdered by their father fifteen years ago."

"Ah," said Alexis, and I supposed that the profession of medium would tend to inure one to violent death among one's interlocutors. "But on Friday... Myra wasn't satisfied. She and Oleander kept pushing, saying they wanted to talk to the other spirit."

"What other spirit?" I said.

"I don't know!" The words burst out of him, leaving us both taken aback. Alexis recovered first. "I know there are other spirits who don't speak—there always are—but I don't know their names. And I don't know who it is that Myra wants to find. I asked her afterwards if it was old T. Zacharias, and she said not to be dense. But she kept asking, and Oleander kept asking, and they never got an answer. Myra says it's just nerves making me think something strange is going on, but it isn't. I know better than that. That's why I want your help."

"*My* help?"

"You're an archivist," he began impatiently, and at that most inauspicious of moments, I heard footsteps in the hall: two or three men and the hard clatter of a woman's shoes.

"Damnation," Alexis said. "I didn't think they'd be this fast."

"Are you sure—"

But the footsteps halted outside my door, and Dr Starkweather, as per usual, came in without knocking. He was accompanied by Captain and Mrs Blackburn, and by Marcus Oleander, who was as shining and repellant as ever.

"*Darling!*" said Myra Blackburn, enveloping Alexis in an embrace I could not help seeing as proprietary. "We've been so *worried!*"

"Mr Booth," said Captain Blackburn, striding across the room and seizing my hand in a hearty grip before I could evade him, "thank you for looking after Alexis for us." Behind him, Dr Starkweather was glaring at me like a double-barrelled shotgun. He hated being interrupted in the middle of the day, and he had clearly taken a violent dislike to Mr Oleander and the Blackburns. And I was clearly the easiest person to blame.

"I, er—"

"He does get these silly notions sometimes," Mrs Blackburn chimed in, her arm around Alexis. "Really, Alexis, you ought to know better than to bother poor Mr Booth when he's working."

"I, er, I didn't mind," I said feebly.

"Now, Mr Booth," Dr Starkweather said with a jovial laugh as false as fool's gold.

"It's very kind of you, but I think we've imposed on the museum quite long enough." Mrs Blackburn swept Alexis and her husband out.

Marcus Oleander lingered in the doorway to ask, "Will we see you at the weekend, Mr Booth?"

I glanced at Dr Starkweather, who said, "Of course you will! Hate to leave a job unfinished, don't you, Mr Booth?"

"…Yes, sir," I said, and Mr Oleander smirked and sauntered away. I could almost imagine I saw the glistening trail he left, like a slug.

Then Dr Starkweather said awfully, "*Well*, Mr Booth?" and I braced myself for the typhoon.

FOR THE REST of Wednesday—once I had escaped Dr Starkweather's wrath—and all of Thursday, I abandoned Mr Lucent and the box from the North Lobby coat check to their fates and went prospecting in the stacks for information about T. Zacharias Tull and Thirdhop Scarp. If Alexis wanted an archivist's help, I could not imagine what else he would have had in mind. And in all honesty, it was a relief to have an excuse to go looking.

I found myself, almost immediately, reading about Zenobia Webster Tull, T. Zacharias Tull's even more infamous mother, and the person for whom Thirdhop Scarp was built.

She had broken with Spiritualism decisively in the early days of her marriage, and Thirdhop Scarp had been intended partly as a center for occultist study, whatever exactly "occultism" was. The definition seemed to change to suit Mrs Tull's mood—and I did not forget that Myra Blackburn was apparently now calling Tullite occultism necromancy. The house had therefore been as much an expression of Zenobia Webster Tull's personality as anything else, and once it was built, she never went anywhere else for more than a week or two at a time. She had borne all but one of her children there.

And all but one had died there as well.

I tracked down their deaths, one by one. Emily Tull died at the age of seven, and she died horribly: she fell into the fireplace in the drawing room, and her burns finally killed her almost a week later. Cecilia drowned in the ornamental lake when she was forty. Randolph fell down the servants' stair and broke his neck. Agnes Tull committed suicide. And Violet Tull Godfrey, the only one of the six who married, died in a New York hospital of primly unspecified complications in her second pregnancy.

Zenobia Webster Tull died of a stroke when she was seventy-five. Although three of her children survived her, she left everything to T. Zacharias. Even her single grandchild, Christabel, received nothing. I traced the connection, from the obituary of Violet Tull Godfrey, "survived by her husband, John Everhart Godfrey, and her daughter Christabel," to the announcement of Christabel Godfrey's wedding in the most cosmopolitan of the city's papers. She had married a man named Conrad Hallett and in the fullness of time became Marcus Oleander's guest in her grandmother's house.

T. Zacharias Tull, his mother's heir in all senses, had believed, following her, that speaking with the dead, as Spiritualism sought to do, was merely the first step, that through the dead, one could find and command unimaginable power. Ultimately, said T. Zacharias Tull, one could become a god. In the one picture of him I found, he was a withered old man with a face like a sour turtle. He had died in the house at Thirdhop Scarp, suffering a heart attack in the attic, of all places; his body was not found for nearly three days.

Unlike Marcus Oleander, Tull had been secretive about his followers; I was unable to confirm Myra Blackburn among his disciples—if, of course, Myra Blackburn was her real name. For that matter, I found no mention of Marcus Oleander. What I could glean about Tull's teachings, however, was enough to make me sure that if Mrs Blackburn was claiming to be his student, her approach to the occult would be, not merely necromantic, but based on a rhetoric of conquest and compulsion that did not seem to me to be either respectful or safe. Alexis was right to be worried.

But when I reached Thirdhop Scarp, Alexis was not worried at all. His smooth dark surface was undisturbed, nothing sharp, nothing vivid, none of the anxiety I had witnessed on Wednesday. He was politely pleased to see me, apologized gracefully for having "bothered" me, and met my one attempt to talk to him about the house with such studied blankness that I was reduced to stammering incoherence and fled the room.

It was unfortunate, for I was more convinced than ever that something was very wrong. The house seemed almost awake—awake and watching. Saturday afternoon, I found myself humming "Bleu, Jaune, Vert," the French folksong I was listening for a child's voice to sing: Louisa Cathcart, who had been five years old when her father hacked her to pieces. Although I am rarely afflicted by restlessness when working, at that moment I found I could no longer sit still. Leaving my make-work, I forayed into the shelves for books that had belonged to T. Zacharias Tull. They were an interesting and rather unsettling assortment. Witchcraft, demonology, necromancy—there seemed to be nothing at the less salubrious end of the esoteric spectrum in which Tull had *not* been interested. His copy of the 1888 *Book of Whispers* had "Pure poppycock!" emblazoned forthrightly across the title page. A privately printed monograph on the voodoo practices of New Orleans stood next to a French volume which I put down hastily after the barest glance. I had not known Tull was interested in *that*.

And then there were his mother's works, a solid row of them and, if I remembered her bibliography correctly, complete. I took down her rarest book, *The Dwelling of Souls: The Spirits of Places and How to Speak to Them*. She devoted an entire chapter to water spirits, another to the spirits of battlefields. She used the term "*genius loci*" freely, though I could not quite tell in my glancing perusal whether she genuinely meant it as the Romans would have understood it, or whether for her this was simply another means of talking to and about the dead.

The last third of the book dealt with how one might go about *creating* a genium loci, and here she was quite alarmingly methodical and practical in the instructions she gave: which particular kinds of wood and stone to use and how many windows should be positioned facing east. There was a section on the use of blood in laying foundation stones that I skipped over with a shudder. I wondered if Thirdhop Scarp had been built according to these highly eccentric specifications, and if so, how on earth she had convinced the architect to cooperate. From what I remembered of Phythias Ormont's sadly brief career, he had been innovative and of rather dubious mental stability—perhaps he would have considered it an interesting challenge.

And perhaps he had repented of it?

My eye fell on a sentence which began, "A spirit may be bound to a specific place through the use of an object which partakes of the nature of both," and I closed the book more sharply than was necessary. I put it carefully back in its place before returning to my work. And I did not hum, the rest of the afternoon.

That night, I was no longer able to escape my doom: Oleander and the Order Aurorae Aeternae browbeat me into attending their séance. It was an unmistakably concerted effort, and I was so unnerved by the thought that they might have *planned* it that I was unable to defend myself even as poorly as I had before. I was down to nothing but obstinacy, and then Alexis said quietly, "Please, Mr Booth. As a favor to me?"

I knew that he was manipulating me, although he was probably not aware that I knew. But knowing and resisting were two very different things, and I proved no stronger now than I had ever been. And there was a part of me that remembered the fear and underlying anger that I had seen on Wednesday and could not help but wonder if under the surface of manipulation might lie sincerity.

I was a fool, and I knew it. But I went all the same.

And I was rewarded, if one should call it that, by being seated on Alexis's left when we took our places around Zenobia Webster Tull's "séance table" in the drawing room. His fingers were warm and dry and very bony, far preferable to Mrs Hallett's ring-encrusted grip on my left hand. I steadied and slowed my breathing, and prepared to wait the séance out.

There was a lengthy rodomontade about purifying the room, which followed none of the protocols for purification with which I was familiar. Marcus Oleander gave a blessing, gracefully non-specific as to the deity or deities involved. Myra Blackburn spoke an invocation that disturbed me greatly because bits of it sounded familiar from my research that week into the teachings of the Tulls, *mère et fils*. I was the more disturbed because her invocation seemed to be using certain terms interchangeably (the caller, the seeker, the vessel), which was either dangerously sloppy—something I did not for a moment believe of Myra Blackburn—or indicative of some second purpose lurking beneath the banal surface of the invocation like a monster beneath the placid surface of... of an ornamental lake.

I acknowledged to myself that I was overwrought. But I remembered an encounter I had had with the genuine *Book of Whispers*, and the use of the word "vessel" was not a happy presagement of Myra Blackburn's intentions.

All in all, I was almost relieved when Alexis finally began the séance proper. It was obvious that he had been taught by Mrs Blackburn—and that he was accustomed to performance—for he spoke at length, and very dramatically, before he invited the spirits to speak.

Most mediums had a "guide" or "control"—a spirit who came with them from séance to séance and acted as something between a tour guide and a primary school teacher, organizing and monitoring the interactions between the living and the dead. The guide also ensured, of course, that the séance-goers would get *something*, even if the rest of the séance was a failure. I had heard Mrs Blackburn telling Mrs Hallett that Alexis's gifts as a medium were so great that he did not need an intermediary, and I found myself, as I watched Alexis sidelong without raising my head, wondering uncomfortably how a person came by such "gifts," for my own experience with the occult had taught me that there were no true gifts, only bargains made before one fully realized what one was trading away.

But perhaps Alexis was a cannier bargainer than I.

The silence held for a long time, as thick and soft as

fog, and then a voice said, not Alexis's, "Why are you here?"

It was a high-pitched voice; although it was perfectly audible, I could not categorize it as anything but "faint," as if it were speaking from a great distance, or with great difficulty, or somehow both. I thought it was a child's voice, although I was not sure. It could also have been the voice of a madwoman. The tone was completely unreadable.

"We are friends," Mrs Hallett said.

"Friends," said the voice. "Whose friends? *My* friends?"

"Who are you?" asked Mr Kitchener.

There was no answer, although the tune of "Bleu, Jaune, Vert" drifted through the room. Was this Louisa, then? But if it was, where were her sisters?

"Who are you?" Mr Kitchener said again.

"No one," the voice said, with a high, horrible giggle. "Dead and gone, dead and gone."

"Who *were* you?" Mr Kitchener persisted, but the voice did not answer.

"Try again, Alexis," Mrs Blackburn murmured.

Alexis's hand tightened on mine; he muttered something under his breath, and the voice, child or madwoman, said, "What do you want?" It sounded distressed.

"D-don't frighten her," I whispered.

Mr Merridew managed a scoffing laugh, although not a very good one. "She's a ghost. What does she have to be frightened of?"

The fireplace at the far end of the room came to life with a roar. There was no fire laid, but the flames were plainly visible from where I sat. There were some cries of shock, and those with their backs to the fireplace twisted around, and thus we were all watching when a child—

vague, blurry, much less vivid than the fire—appeared in front of the fireplace.

The next second, the child fell into the flames. She became much more sharply visible as she fell; I saw her dress catch fire. I had been wrong. She was not Louisa Cathcart. I knew that she was Emily Tull, that she would linger in terrible pain for most of a week before she died. And her ghost would be trapped here, singing "Bleu, Jaune, Vert," as she must have been singing that afternoon, always coming back to this moment, the fire, the helpless agony.

I do not know if we all screamed. I know that I did and that the circle broke apart as two or three persons lunged uselessly for the fireplace—which, on the instant, was bare and cold again. The flames were gone and the ghostly child with them.

There were several minutes of unedifying chaos.

Someone had the presence of mind to go find the brandy decanter and pour a measure for each of us. I prefer to avoid alcohol as a rule, but I did not hesitate— although I could not drain my glass in a swallow as some of the others did. My wits cleared, and I realized that while most of the Order was clustered near the door, clamoring around Marcus Oleander and Myra Blackburn, Alexis was still sitting in the chair to my right, his back very straight and his face perfectly calm, if rather too pale.

I myself was huddled in my chair like a broken umbrella; I straightened and said cautiously to Alexis, "Are you, er, all right?"

"Fine," he said, although it was a transparent lie. "Mr Booth, what *was* that?"

"Have you never seen anything like that before?"

"Not exactly," he said, with a sidelong look. Then, as if recollecting himself, he said, "No. Never."

I did not want to know what he had seen, so I did not rise to his bait. I said, "That was what killed Emily Tull. She was Zenobia Webster Tull's second child, and she died when she was seven."

"She fell into the fireplace?" Alexis said, and I thought perhaps his wide-eyed horror was genuine.

"Yes. She died six days later."

"Oh God."

"It answers the question of what the dead have to fear," I said—perhaps a trifle dourly, for I did not like Mr Merridew.

"It wasn't Emily last time, so I didn't know—I would have been more careful if—"

"I don't see what precautions you could have taken," I said.

"If we think there's likely to be a problem, Myra asks the questions and we don't let anyone else speak. But last time, it was fine! It was an older girl. She wouldn't give us her name, but she talked about the rose garden with Miss Parrington. She named all the roses."

She *had* been giving them her name, I thought, for surely that had been Rose Cathcart. I found myself reluctant to tell Alexis that small secret, and indeed I would barely have had the opportunity to do so, for the next moment, Mrs Blackburn was there, pulling Alexis out of his chair and saying loudly that too many demands had been made on the medium this evening.

I saw their eyes meet in perfect complicity, then Alexis stumbled, letting Mrs Blackburn support him, and they staged a small but very effective drama all the way to the door—and doubtless up the stairs as well. When they made their exit, their audience followed them. I retreated in the opposite direction, to the library, for it was futile to imagine I would sleep. I locked the doors and decided arbitrarily that tonight would be a good time to examine the catalogues of the two libraries Marcus Oleander had inherited—or bought, if Alexis was telling the truth, and I thought that in this instance he might be.

The two catalogues, and the collections they represented, could not have been more different. One was a true catalogue raisonné, with detailed entries for each book including both the bibliographic information and a description of the actual object. The other was more of a day-book, with titles scribbled down as they were purchased and crossed out as they were sold again. The catalogue raisonné might not turn out to be any more accurate, but it was far more pleasant to work with.

Moreover, the collection it described, while somewhat eccentric, was carefully researched and nicely judged. There was no place for Isaiah Hope Turnbull here, and a number of volumes, while minor, were items I would have been glad to acquire for the Parrington. Mr Abel Ditney, whoever he had been, had been a scholar who loved his work and took pride in it. I found that I was sorry I would never have the chance to correspond with him.

The day-book, on the other hand, in the cramped, somehow mumbling writing of one Bartholomew Stanes Harcourt, Esquire, recorded the purchases of a man who believed in nearly everything, haphazardly and without any distinction made between a pirated 1583 quarto of Carolus Albinus (the Bohemian necromancer's first publication in England) and a pamphlet printed in 1882 which purported to teach one how to banish ancient

Roman spirits from one's belligerently jingoistic English home. I got letters from men like this, and they always made me feel uneasily as if there were a spider crawling on my collar.

I sat and looked despairingly at the efforts of Mr Ditney and Mr Stanes Harcourt. I knew it was worse than useless to begin any sort of work with their catalogues until I had completed my own, but at that moment, I felt that if I wrote another catalogue card, I would go simply, quietly, irretrievably mad. Yet I knew that if I went to bed, I would only lie awake, listening to every sound the house made in the night and seeing on my closed eyelids the flames leaping in an empty fireplace.

Then, as if in answer to an incoherent prayer, I thought of a task that, while inefficient to tackle now, was not actually useless or worse. Finding duplicate volumes—of which there were certain to be several—would genuinely make matters easier later on. It provided an excuse both to roam the shelves and to dig through the crates, and although I would need to make notes, it would not require another catalogue card.

I have a better memory for book titles than I do for names; it was easy and pleasant work to look through the crates and boxes of Mr Ditney and Mr Stanes Harcourt's libraries and pull out books for which I knew I had written a card. Twice I caught myself humming "Bleu, Jaune, Vert," but that was not so dreadful, and I made myself stop.

I made very light penciled notations on the flyleaf of each duplicate I found: AD, BSH, MO, or TZT. That way, even if the collections got mixed up—and one of the things I dreaded was the possibility of returning to Thirdhop Scarp one Friday and discovering the Order

Aurorae Aeternae had gotten into the library—it would still be possible to keep the Ditney and Tull collections intact. As the night wore on, I ended up writing catalogue cards anyway, as some of the duplicates, being from different printings, had idiosyncrasies that it seemed better to note now than to come back to.

One such was the *De Primordia Rerum* of Conrad Oettinger, a book notable for the three consecutive printings in which, while one error was corrected, another as bad or worse was introduced. Mr Ditney had clearly been amused or intrigued—or both—by this chain of incompetence and ill-luck, for he had acquired the complete run of printings, from the first to the belated, error-free fifth. I was paging through T. Zacharias Tull's copy to find out which printing it was, mostly occupied with trying to think of a way to make Marcus Oleander understand that he should keep Mr Ditney's five Oettingers together, when my eye was caught by a marginal notation in T. Zacharias Tull's distinctive italic script.

It was the section on purgation by fire, with its discussion of the burning of heretics and witches compared with the ancient Greek practice of burnt offerings, and with additional notes on the use of funeral pyres by the Germanic tribes. It was a particularly unpleasant section in a book that was by and large harmless, and it always made me grateful that Oettinger had not known about the Hindu practice of suttee.

T. Zacharias Tull had made a number of notes around *Lustratio igni,* most of them incomprehensible, as anyone's notes to himself are likely to be to someone else, but this one was all too clear. Next to the paragraph about strength being carried through the fire from the victim to the person making the offering—it was Oettinger's opinion that Queen Mary I had sickened and died because she had not burned a sufficient number of Protestants, or at least had not personally attended a sufficient number of burnings—Tull had written, *NOT TRUE*. Then, later (a finer nib and a slightly different shade of ink) he had added, ? *Did not die in fire.*

I slammed the book shut as if I were killing a venomous insect. I had to grit my teeth against nausea, and I realized I could hear Emily Tull with perfect clarity, her tuneless child's voice singing "Bleu, Jaune, Vert" as if she were wandering among the bookshelves.

But I did not need that oblique confirmation. I knew. T. Zacharias Tull had murdered his sister when she was seven years old. He would have been eleven? Twelve? He had murdered her, and as an adult, he had coolly assessed her murder in the light of Oettinger's theories.

If I had been able to leave Thirdhop Scarp at that instant, I would have done so, and unlike Lot's wife, would have felt no temptation to look back. But it was the middle of the night; I had neither anywhere I could go nor any means of getting there. And Dr Starkweather would only make me return.

I sat for some time with my elbows on the table and my face in my hands, listening unwillingly as the child's voice slowly faded into silence. When I checked my watch, it was a quarter after three. It seemed even more unlikely that I would be able to sleep, but I was repulsed by the company of T. Zacharias Tull's books. I could lie quietly in bed and rehearse arguments I would never use for why Dr Starkweather should not send me back to Thirdhop Scarp.

The idea was an attractive one. I tidied my materials

away, and my hand was mere inches from the doorknob when I remembered last weekend: the damp, persistent *something* that had pawed at the door. What if it was out there now? What if it was on its way?

I held my breath, listening. Though I heard nothing, I could not entirely convince myself that silence meant nothing was there. It was foolish to hover here, frightened of what was almost certainly an empty hallway, but I could not dismiss the memory of that stagnant smell, or of the sounds it had made as it labored to get in.

I retreated to the table and spent the rest of the night, ears straining for a noise which never came, writing catalogue cards for Mr Ditney's books.

THAT SUNDAY, MARCUS Oleander did not appear to bid me farewell, but I was not short of company. A number of the Order Aurorae Aeternae were making their departure from Thirdhop Scarp. I was wedged between one of the women, who appeared as if she had been awake crying all night, and Mr Merridew, who looked scarcely any better. The woman's husband—I could not think of their names—kept casting anxious glances at his wife.

Mr Merridew tried to start a conversation, but the husband returned only uninterested monosyllables, and the wife did not even seem to hear him. For my part, I could find no answers; I have no gift for small-talk, and I was afraid that anything I said would later be used to mock me. It was a relief to reach the station, where we parted, for they were traveling first class and I was traveling second.

I cannot sleep in public places, but my thoughts were

slow and disjointed all the way back to the city. I thought about Emily Tull and the restlessness in the house that morning—there had been strange sighing noises in the stairwell, and the curtains in the breakfast parlor had billowed gently throughout the meal although the windows were shut. There had been a knock at my bedroom door three times while I was changing my clothes, and no one at all in the hallway. My thoughts kept circling back to the thing that smelled of lake water, the thing that might or might not have been lurking outside the library doors, and just as the train was pulling into Van Eyck Station, I thought, as sharp and hard as being struck on the head, *Cecilia*. Cecilia Tull had drowned in the ornamental lake, and I was dreadfully certain that T. Zacharias Tull had murdered her, too.

Oettinger, I remembered, had advised against sacrifice by water.

On Thursday, the news was in all the papers: Paul Merridew had committed suicide by jumping off the Cyrus Street Bridge. The Cyrus Street Bridge was a particular favorite with suicides, and I knew without looking that there would be another round of the same old dreary editorial debate, with one editor demanding the bridge be closed to foot traffic, another decrying the inability of the police to do their jobs, and a third finding in Mr Merridew's death confirmation of the hobby horse of the moment, whether that was the unnaturalness of women working outside the home or the iniquity of the latest tax proposed by the city. They might remember to offer a few platitudes about the grief of the living—did Paul Merridew leave anyone to grieve for him?—but they would not waste even a line wondering what had driven the unhappy creature to his death.

I did not delude myself that I could have changed his fate by talking with him on Sunday, but I knew I would always wonder what he might have said if given the chance. Had he, too, dreamed of being imprisoned in Thirdhop Scarp?

On Friday, Dr Starkweather called me into his office and informed me that Miss Parrington had left Thirdhop Scarp and was currently planning a trip to India. I found his self-congratulatory tone both unearned and in very poor taste, but I was too grateful to mind. I worked late that evening, glad even of my office's manifold inconveniences and filled with hope that I might never have to think about Thirdhop Scarp again.

IV

It was a forlorn hope from the beginning, as I had not taken into account Marcus Oleander's desire to be seen as a man of letters. For more than a month, however, and with Dr Starkweather's good will, I was able to put him off, truthfully pleading a nearly Biblical inundation of work, as a pair of life-long antiquarians and bibliophiles died—as surely they would have wished—within three days of each other; they left both their joint collection and their quite extensive individual collections to the Parrington. I was working late each night and most of the weekends as well. I could not have gone to Thirdhop Scarp if I had wished to.

I tried to put the house and its denizens entirely out of my mind, with luck which ranged from excellent to poor. I did not help myself, either, by my inability to stay away from Paul Merridew's funeral. It was a small, dismal affair, unpublicized; I could not even explain to myself why I felt it necessary to go. I did not know any of the mourners—none of the Order Aurorae Aeternae whom I had met chose to attend—and there was nothing, neither absolution nor answers nor anything else, to be found in the varnished surface of the casket. I felt like a vulture; in penance, I forced myself to offer my condolences to Paul Merridew's sister, the only family member left to survive him.

She was small, pale, very fragile, with violet circles shadowing her dark eyes, and fine dark brown hair that would not stay pinned beneath her hat. I told her my name, and felt her surprise in the small gloved hand she had presented to me. "Paul mentioned you! You were at Thirdhop Scarp last... the last time he was there."

"I, er..."

"But you're not a member of the Order."

It was half a question, and I said, "No," thankfully.

"Then maybe you will be honest with me. Mr Booth, do you think Mr Oleander is responsible for Paul's death?"

"I don't know why your brother, er, chose as he did."

"He left a note," she said, and to my horror, she fumbled it out of her small handbag and pressed it into my hands. "It doesn't make any sense to me, but maybe it will to you."

Dear Felicia (the note ran), *I did not know it would be like this. I thought the dead would*

There, a word, which looked to me like *forgive*, had been scratched out, and the sentence finished, *be at peace. I'm sorry, but I can't*

And there the scrawling letters trailed off entirely, as if he had not been able to find the word he needed. Some way down the page, an even more wretched scrawl reiterated, *I'm sorry*, and then there was a squiggle that I assumed was *Paul*.

I understood part of what he was writing about, for there could be no doubt that Emily Tull was not at peace. Nor, I thought, had she forgiven her murderer. But Paul Merridew had not known that she had been murdered or that she had anyone to forgive.

It was not *her* forgiveness he had been seeking in Marcus Oleander's train.

"Did he, er, was there someone he knew who died? Someone he might have wanted forgiveness from?"

"I don't know," she said. "Well, there was a friend. At school. He committed suicide... too." I waited while she composed herself. "But I don't know why Paul would be worried about Freddy."

I could think of all too many possible reasons, but if Felicia Merridew did not know them, it would be no kindness to enlighten her. "We, er... sometimes we worry about strange things. And it's always worse with... with something like this."

"Suicide, you mean," she said, daring me to protest.

"Yes," I agreed humbly. "I'm sorry, Miss Merridew."

She stared at me as the rising wind blew strands of her hair across her face. Then she nodded. "Thank you, Mr Booth. It was kind of you to come."

It was not kind, and it had done neither her nor me any good. I left the cemetery and stalked back to the Parrington, determined yet again to put Thirdhop Scarp out of my mind. I was at least partially successful, in that for the next few weeks, I had no spare time in which to torment myself. But Marcus Oleander's persistent inquiries were uncomfortable, and I was not reassured by the news that Miss Parrington had not, after all, gone to India, but merely to a cousin's cabin in the Adirondacks, whence she returned some six weeks after Paul Merridew's death as eagerly and earnestly thoughtless as ever. This information I had from a fellow curator who had the ill luck to cross her path, and from that point on, I think I was almost expecting the blow which fell the following Thursday: Miss Parrington was returning to Thirdhop Scarp that weekend, and Mrs Crowe desired me to do the same.

It was with no small bitterness that I packed my bag on Friday. I regarded the second-class coach with loathing, and all but snarled at the Pittmanville train station and the waiting automobile. I managed to be civil to the chauffeur, who was again restfully silent, but forcing myself out of the automobile at Thirdhop Scarp's grand front door was very difficult, especially as Marcus Oleander was standing on the front steps waiting for me with a wide, white smile.

If he knew or guessed that my movements were dictated by Miss Parrington's, he gave no sign; his welcome was as untrustworthy and fulsome as ever, and he conducted me to the library with a number of anxious questions: was I comfortable? did I need better light? more catalogue cards? should he send one of the maids to help? I declined this last with more force than politeness and then had to regroup. Alienating Marcus Oleander would not help anything. "Everything's fine," I assured him, although I was lying. "It's just…" I groped, floundered, and managed something that was at least truthful: "This, er, process simply takes a great deal of time. There's no way… that is, I can't make it quicker."

"And of course you have your own work," he said, which was most likely a dig at my lengthy absence. "I only wish I could afford to pay you."

I wished that, too, but did not say so. I opened the library doors, mumbled something fatuous about soonest begun, soonest done, and if I did not close the door in Marcus Oleander's face, it was only because he was not standing near enough. I was afraid for a moment that he might pursue me—it was, after all, *his* library, and I could hardly deny him entrance—but he did not, and I was able to turn my attention to the books.

My loathing for T. Zacharias Tull had not lessened, but in daylight it was easier to remember that the books were only books, not manifestations of their former owner. I worked steadily until the sun sank far enough that it was shining in my eyes, a reminder to look at my watch; it lacked only an hour before I would have to change for dinner. Although I was tempted simply to move my chair and keep working—and perhaps forgo dinner altogether—common sense pointed out that this was a bad idea. Furthermore, I might (as my colleagues frequently accused me) be determined to work myself into an early grave, but I did not want to do so *here*. I tidied my things away and went to walk in the gardens for an hour.

I was not paying any particular attention either to my surroundings or my direction, but I had certainly not intended to go anywhere near the ornamental lake; thus, I was dismayed to find myself standing, not on the gravel path beside it, but actually on the bank, in an unpleasantly boggy spot—as if the lake were trying to expand, although I had no idea if lakes did such things. I had no clear memory of how I had come there.

I startled backwards and something turned beneath my foot. I was unable to save myself from a fall. It would have been humiliating if I had not been so frightened or if, when I looked to see what had tripped me, I had not found a nasty tangle of bones and matted fur—the remains of what had once been a squirrel cached here in a stand of tall grass.

I lurched to my feet, nearly falling again before I made it to the path. I was on the verge of bolting back to the house like a hunted deer when a voice said sternly, "After dark, you should not be here."

I slewed around, having to stagger to stay upright, and beheld the limping approach of a very elderly man. The mud stains on his shabby plus-fours and tweed jacket suggested he was the gardener, and the fierce light in his pale blue eyes suggested even more strongly that, whatever Marcus Oleander might claim to the newspapers, the gardens of Thirdhop Scarp did not suffer from his inspiration.

"Yes," I said. "I mean, no. That is... you're perfectly right."

"Good," he said. It was almost *güt*.

"I found a dead thing," I blurted and was mortified. There was no reason to tell him; there was nothing he could do. And it did not make me look any less a fool.

"Ach," the old man said, sounding both disgusted and exasperated, but not in the least surprised. "A bird this time, is it? A rabbit?"

"A squirrel. I think." I pointed to the stand of tall grass where I had fallen, and the old man stumped over to look, muttering under his breath.

When he straightened again, he looked no happier than I felt, and he flapped his hands at me as if I were a flock of pigeons. "Go on with you! It is only another dead creature. There is no need to be lingering over the bones."

Truly, I wanted nothing more than to retreat to the house, but... "*Another* dead creature?"

"Ever since I am coming here," he said, regaining the path with an effort, "small dead things I am finding— one a month, two a month. Now it is more. Two, three a week. First the little ones, the shrews and voles. Then squirrels, birds, rabbits. Woodchucks. Raccoons. Once a cat, and her I bury far away from here. I tell Mr Oleander to tell guests not to bring dogs, and he remembers the carp, how they vanish, and he listens."

"But what do you think is doing it?" I had my own answer, although I was unwilling to speak her name aloud.

"I do not know," the old man said, pale blue eyes meeting mine forthrightly, and I knew he lied.

THE GARDENER'S NAME was Hans Friedrich Jürgens. He might have been German, Swiss, or Austrian; I would have wagered fairly confidently on German, and I did not ask. He walked with me back to the house, almost as if he were shepherding me, and he told me about his roses at great length, with obvious pride, and so unstoppably that I had no second chance to ask about the ornamental lake and the "small dead things." And Cecilia.

When I entered the house, Mr Oleander was waiting for me at the foot of the stairs, his eyebrows raised. "I see you've made a conquest," he said. "I didn't think old Jürgens knew that many words of English."

"He was telling me about the roses," I said stiffly and added, although I knew I should not, "in German." It was perfectly true: Herr Jürgens had slipped once, looked quickly at me—checking, I thought, merely to be certain that I was not going to start ranting about "krauts." When I said, "I understand German, although I do not speak it," he beamed at me in open delight, and I did not have the heart to tell him I knew nothing whatsoever about roses.

Mr Oleander opened his mouth for some no doubt scathing yet witty remark; I said, "I'm going to be late. Excuse me." I brushed past him and escaped up the stairs.

I expected my reprieve to be no more than temporary, but when I came downstairs again, I found that matters at Thirdhop Scarp had changed dramatically since I had last been there. Mr Oleander had no time to spare for baiting me; he was too desperately involved in the struggle to keep his kingdom from crumbling away beneath his feet.

The same number of guests sat around the shining mahogany table, and there were some of the same faces. But others were new to me, and I realized quickly that they were not of the same caliber as the people I had encountered previously at Thirdhop Scarp, although it took me longer to pinpoint the difference. Miss Parrington was there, of course, and utterly unchanged. The Halletts were there again; knowing, as I now did, that Christabel Hallett was the last surviving descendent of Zenobia Webster Tull, I observed her more carefully, and I began to see that, while she obviously admired Marcus Oleander, she was not innocent of ulterior motives. Even as she flattered him, she was trying to extract some sort of concession from him, pushing an agenda which I was not familiar enough with the works of Zenobia Webster Tull to decipher, but which seemed to have to do with a different interpretation of some of the Order Aurorae Aeternae's central teachings. Oleander avoided her attacks adroitly, but I noticed that some of his guests were listening to Mrs Hallett, and listening very carefully.

Chief among them was Agnes Quincey. Miss Quincey was the person primarily responsible for the Order

Aurorae Aeternae's city activities, the séances and salons and the already infamous Halloween ball. She was short and stout, both cheerful and ferociously decisive; I had observed women like her among the Parrington's docents, and I knew they, rather than their gentle, ineffective, "ladylike" sisters, were the ones who ran the museum's volunteers. I was grateful for their existence and avoided them as much as possible.

But from watching them, I knew enough to identify Miss Quincey's frustration. She was eager for more responsibility, more authority, in the Order Aurorae Aeternae, access to its more esoteric secrets, and Marcus Oleander would not give it to her. I watched him with his female disciples, and I saw that while he was delighted by their attention and gratified by their loyalty, he did not regard them as anything more than a chorus of admiration. For serious discussion, he turned to the men. The only woman he seemed to respect was Myra Blackburn, and that was only because she forced it upon him.

He was turning a strength into a weakness, for these women had a great reserve of time, energy, and talent which they were desperately eager to put at his service. By denying them the opportunity, he not only stagnated the Order Aurorae Aeternae, he left his flank grievously exposed, for Mrs Hallett's rhetoric was not falling on deaf ears. I caught snatches of it all through dinner, and the warm responses of Miss Quincey and Mrs Seftick. They were very willing to consider the claims of Zenobia Webster Tull's heir. Thus, the women were forming an alliance under Marcus Oleander's nose while he was preoccupied with the sphinx-like Myra Blackburn, and the men quarreled endlessly and bitterly.

Michael Kitchener's jealousy of his status as Marcus Oleander's lieutenant, which I had noticed before Paul Merridew's death, was only becoming worse the longer Oleander persisted in his pursuit of Myra Blackburn, and it was exacerbated by the presence of Miss Quincey and the Sefticks and especially Patterson Bell.

Even I knew the name of Patterson Bell. He was a wealthy man—his father and uncles and at least one of his brothers had been associates of my guardian, and of a far greater luster than J. A. Cathcart—and he had spent the first fifty years of his life in the blameless, respectable, and unremarkable acquisition of greater wealth. Then his eldest son disappeared in the war. No one knew what had happened to Leyland Bell; his body was never found, and Patterson Bell, having exhausted all the mundane means of searching, became interested in the occult. He went from séance to séance, planchette to table tipping, trying to get an answer, a solution. He was widely credulous, although he retained his shrewdness about human beings, so that he was only very rarely taken in by outright frauds. But no matter how many charlatans he encountered and recognized, he never lost his faith that the answers he sought could be found via psychics or mediums or clairvoyants.

Between his wealth and his acumen, Patterson Bell represented an achievement for Marcus Oleander, and it was apparent that Michael Kitchener was consumed by bitter envy, that he wanted Oleander to notice him in the way he noticed Bell. There was nothing necessarily sexual about his jealousy, only that desperate desire, which I think we all must learn in childhood, to have our idol smile at us. Little though I liked Michael Kitchener, I could not help sympathizing with his baffled frustration.

I had enough experience of the phenomenon to parse the situation: Kitchener had been the recipient of Oleander's confidences; he had been encouraged to believe that there was a special understanding between them which no one else would ever share. Now, though, Oleander was talking in that intimate way to Bell, making a show of excluding Kitchener—and that did not even recognize the influence of Myra Blackburn, like a malign star. Kitchener could not understand what had changed, and he could neither contrive a return to the *status quo ante* nor accept that there was no way back.

If Oleander was merely stupid and self-defeating in his treatment of his female disciples, I thought he was actively courting danger in playing games with the volatile Kitchener. Kitchener was not like me, to accept any quantity of neglect and mockery in return for a few crumbs of affection. All that was saving Oleander from serious and violent rifts in the Order Aurorae Aeternae was Kitchener's jealousy. He would not make common cause with Agnes Quincey or Patterson Bell so long as he perceived them to be threats to the position he believed he held. But that state of affairs could not last forever. Let Kitchener become even marginally more hostile to Myra Blackburn, and he would ally himself with Agnes Quincey and the ambitions of Christabel Hallett. At that point, Oleander's ability to control his followers would evaporate, and if Oleander himself did not realize it, Myra Blackburn certainly did. I wondered if that was her aim.

The atmosphere around the dinner table was uncomfortable, but at least no one had any attention to spare for me. I was glad to be insignificant.

The servants were clearing away the last of the plates, prior to bringing out the coffee service, and I was wondering if I could possibly slip away unnoticed before anyone tried to organize me into the evening's activities, whatever they might be. I remember it distinctly because I had just ascertained that Oleander and his guests were all in the dining room—no one unaccounted for whom I might encounter as I escaped—when there was a terrible noise, crashing and screaming all mixed together. Horribly, the scream cut off some moments before the crashing ended.

The entire company was frozen like a waxwork tableau. Then the maid said, "Oh, God, Jim!" She shoved the stack of plates in her hands onto the nearest flat surface and bolted out the door that gave access to the kitchen and the back stairs. She left the door open behind her, and we all clearly heard a man's voice say, "Erna, are you all right? What was that noise?"

"Jim? But I thought—who fell down the stairs?"

"It must've been one of the gentlemen, mustn't it?" And by then the maid had returned to the dining room, followed by a man in chef's whites. They stared at the assembled guests and we stared back, each person visibly counting the assembly and realizing that no one was absent. The silence became peculiarly and dreadfully charged; I felt my hackles rising. Marcus Oleander said, "Donnelly, will you be sure the other servants are accounted for and, ah, unharmed?"

"Yes, sir," said the chef and withdrew. The maid, ashen-faced, picked up the plates and continued clearing the table. Oleander looked around with glittering eyes. I saw excitement in his face—almost triumph.

He said, "Zenobia Webster Tull's second son, Randolph, died in a fall down the stairs. We must have just heard it reenacted, and I think we should investigate. Don't you?"

I was sickened by the speed with which the company agreed. *It is their interest in the occult that drew them to Oleander,* I argued to myself. *Why should they* not *be excited at the chance to investigate a haunting they have witnessed for themselves?* But I kept hearing the way that scream had cut off.

I followed Oleander and the others into the narrow back hallway. The stairs were also narrow, twisting around an odd angle of the house, and despite the electric light, they were dark, every stair casting odd-angled shadows.

Alexis and Mrs Blackburn were murmuring together. I wondered if there was anything genuine in their serious expressions. I watched as the Order Aurorae Aeternae gradually became quieter and quieter, their gazes turning toward Alexis like sunflowers toward the sun. It was true that there was nothing else at which to look: no ghostly body crumpled at the foot of the stairs, no dents in the yellowing plaster of the walls, nothing to indicate that a man had fallen to his death down these stairs.

But we had all heard it happen. I could still hear it if I let myself dwell on it, the terrible chaos, hard and hollow and sharp all at once. I understood, abruptly, the hold that mediums, both fraudulent and real, had on people; they claimed that they could make sense out of senseless pain. Mediums made it look as if there were answers to all questions, and the reason I could never trust them was that I knew there were not, that sometimes the answer only served to make the darkness deeper.

Randolph Tull had died more than thirty years ago. No fairy tale that Alexis could tell would change the fact that we had been helpless witnesses to the death of a man whose bones were crumbling in his grave.

I could not bear to watch Alexis's performance. I

slipped away just as he was saying, "The energies here are very turbulent." No one saw me go, save Alexis himself.

"TURBULENT" WAS A good word to describe Thirdhop Scarp that weekend. There were knockings at people's doors in the middle of the night; apports—stones appearing on sofa cushions, plates breaking themselves against the walls; a persistent cold spot in the front hall, just to the left of the enormous, baroque hatrack. Emily's tuneless singing faded in and out of the library. Randolph's fall repeated itself on Saturday night. Miss Quincey reported hearing a voice beside the window at the end of the hallway on the second floor of the south wing, a woman's voice, calm and rather flat, saying, "He'll never find it now." Unless it was, "We'll never find it now." Alvin Seftick heard a woman crying. He was in the bathroom at the time, but he said the sound was directionless; he knew it was not in the bathroom with him, but that was all. The atmosphere was angry, hostile, although diffusely. The house hated us, I thought in the cold early hours of Sunday morning, but it could not quite *find* us.

I could not sleep, and not in the way to which I was accustomed, the way, familiar my entire life, in which sleep simply was not there. In Thirdhop Scarp that weekend, I could not sleep because every time I closed my eyes, I was suffocating. I would open them, and the bedroom would be quiet and dark around me, cool to the point of chilliness because I had opened the window— just an inch, just enough to feel the bite of the night air. I would take a deep breath, reassure myself that I was not choking, that the bedcovers were not over my face, that the air in the room was brisk and fresh. And then I closed my eyes and was suffocating again.

What was worse than the sleeplessness was that I did not dare work in the library past midnight. I could not clear my memory of that sad, nasty tangle of fur and bones. I could not keep from thinking about what Herr Jürgens had said. *Small dead things.* And I could not convince myself that the thing I had thought I had heard in the hallway all those weeks ago was just imagination. Or that it would not come back.

On Friday night, I tried. I sat in the library and tried to concentrate. But not only did every sound jerk my head up like a marionette's string, I also kept coming back to myself with a jump and discovering that I was staring at the library doors, watching the knobs.

Waiting for one of them to start turning, and what I would do then, I had not the faintest idea.

I must have checked the locks twenty times in the hour between midnight and one. At one o'clock, I admitted defeat. I risked the hallway while I still had the courage to make myself do it and went upstairs to my room. It was plain that the thing from the lake, the thing I had thought was in the hallway, could not climb stairs. Otherwise it would have been prowling the second floor, and it would have found an unlocked door or a wandering guest by now. Thus, I was reasonably certain that I was safe, and as I made sure to lock my door, I had no difficulty in focusing my attention on my reading. But no matter how tired I became, I could not sleep. By three A.M., I would almost rather have faced the thing from the lake if it meant I would be able to sleep afterward. Almost.

The book I had brought for the weekend had been finished Saturday before dawn. I was reluctant to remove books from Thirdhop Scarp's library, even temporarily—although I could not pin down the cause, whether I feared that I would be contaminated with the house's miasma or that the house would identify me as a thief and thus be able to find me, and perhaps the most horrible part of the whole vexed question was that neither idea could be entirely dismissed as morbid imagination.

On the other hand, I knew myself well enough to reject the idea of trying to make it through Saturday night *without* a book. I dithered back and forth most of Saturday evening and finally selected one of the books from Mr Ditney's library as being, as it were, neutral ground.

It was impossible to find a book that did not deal with occult subjects, although I would have preferred to read about almost anything else: taxidermy, for instance, or dried flower arranging, although those were about dead things—*small dead things*—too. I made my choice purely by the width of the spine and ended up with a squat volume entitled *A Theory of Haunting*. It was not comforting reading, but nothing in Thirdhop Scarp's library would have been.

The *Theory*'s author, the Honorable Hazel Maria Roylott, had visited haunted places all over the world. Her theory was that certain places had the property of catching energy in the same way that a rain barrel catches rain. She wrote about sacred places from a number of cultures as examples of what happened when this quality was harnessed properly and then turned her attention to places where it had gone wrong. Both good and bad, all of them were man-made structures; Miss Roylott believed that the natural world always released energy back into the universe. It was humankind's habit of building structures out of dead things that allowed energy to collect.

I wondered about beaver dams, wondered about vengeful ghostly beavers mobbing any bear unfortunate enough to come too close, and then told myself sternly not to be ridiculous.

Miss Roylott asserted—and I supposed I had no reason to doubt her—that a person's death caused a release of energy, and that if the death occurred in one of her pitcher plant buildings, rather than being returned to the cycle of exchange that was the world, the energy would be trapped. She was quite clear that by "energy" she did not mean "soul"; the soul was the structure that gave form to the energy, just as the body was the structure that contained it. She persevered into a complicated analogy which I was too tired to follow fully, about bodies and buildings and the necessity of having form to channel stored energy. I reached the end of Chapter Five and realized that somehow Miss Roylott had persuaded me that some buildings constructed their own rudimentary souls.

If the buildings were working with the energy of violent death, Miss Roylott argued at the beginning of Chapter Six, then the souls they built were correspondingly dark and also hungry, always needing more energy to compensate for the depletion and destruction of souls. (I skimmed a lengthy digression on how sacred places, because the energy they collected was always freely given and never the complete emptying of death, did not develop this avariciousness; I suspected Miss Roylott of a certain wishful naïveté.) These places therefore kept collecting more and more energy; inevitably that energy began to discharge itself in phenomena such as apports and ghost lights. If living persons tapped into that energy, they could create poltergeists—or become mediums, particularly those who worked with planchettes or turning tables or the rapping beloved of the Fox sisters.

The Fox sisters, of course, had been frauds.

Miss Roylott went on to discuss the ways by which a haunted place, having developed a crude soul of its own, would begin to preserve or recreate the souls of the dead. I was in the middle of Chapter Seven and wondering just how much of this I could bring myself to believe when I realized I could hear a woman crying.

A Theory of Haunting bounced off my knee and fell to the floor.

It was not a living woman's voice. It was too diffuse, not just soft but somehow vague, unanchored—quite different in that respect from the focused percussion of Randolph Tull's death. Even if I got up and searched, I knew I would not find the crying woman.

I got up anyway. I would not go downstairs, but I could not believe that this mostly eroded weeping could harm me, and I was curious: might there be a room in Thirdhop Scarp where she would be even slightly clearer?

The sound was too soft to wake a sleeper; when I emerged from my room into the hallway shared by all the guest bedrooms, I could deduce that if there was a focal point for the weeping, it was not in any of the occupied rooms. Moving cautiously, I investigated the two unused bedrooms, but the crying did not change in volume or intensity.

I knew that Marcus Oleander and Michael Kitchener had their bedrooms in the main part of the house, while the servants slept in the north wing. In the interests of discretion, I decided to try the third floor of the south wing first, before venturing into territory where I might find people awake. As soft as the crying was, if it *did* have a focal point, I doubted it carried very far from it. And if it did not have a focal point, then I lost nothing by not invading Oleander's private territory.

I climbed the stairs slowly, doing my best not to let them creak. The third floor of the south wing had been the Tull nursery and schoolroom, as I knew from one of Oleander's self-congratulatory lectures about the history of the house (he had not mentioned the Cathcart nursery at all; I knew from the diagrams published in the newspapers that it had been in the central wing). I pressed lights on and off as I moved through the rooms, noticing that once the Tull children were grown, the rooms had been made over: all the furniture was sized for adults. It was not entirely clear to me what the rooms' purposes had been, possibly because of the dust sheets shrouding everything, until I came to the small room at the south end of the hall, which had clearly been a study, for it contained only a desk and a chair, positioned to take advantage of the window. The cold deluge of moonlight meant there was no need to turn on the light.

And this room was what I had been searching for: the source of the crying.

There was no ghostly lady weeping at the desk; the sound was only infinitesimally louder. But this was where it belonged. This was where it had happened.

Where *what* had happened?

Violent death, said the Honorable Hazel Maria Roylott. And Agnes Tull had committed suicide.

Was this where she had done it? Or where she had decided to do it? The wretched weeping suggested it was.

I sat down at the desk, a graceful if rather spindly

example of its species. It was easy to imagine Agnes Tull writing her perfect copperplate at this desk, and not much more difficult to imagine her despairing. It was a bleak little room; I could not help comparing it to the shrine of Zenobia Webster Tull's parlor/study—she might have trumpeted the call for women's intellectual rights, but she had banished her daughter to the farthest corner of the house.

I slid the desk drawer open. Something rattled in the back. I reached in, and my fingers encountered something sharp. I yelped and pulled back. A thin line of blood, black in the moonlight, welled across the pad of my index finger. I reached in again, more carefully, and this time pulled out a knife.

It was a paring knife, small and sharp, stained black at the join of blade and handle. The stinging pain in my finger attested to how easily the edge would slice through flesh, how little pressure it would take to…

I stared blankly at the black welling line across my left wrist, at the knife gripped in my right hand. The sobbing was louder, closer; if I looked up, I would see her reflection in the window instead of my own.

My fingers spasmed, and the knife jerked out of my hand like a living thing. I did not see where it fell; I was watching the blood dripping off my wrist. One drop a black stain on the desk… two…

As the third drop landed, I woke up.

The verb "woke" is misleading, since I had technically been awake the entire time, and I do not mean to imply that I had been sleepwalking or hypnotized or anything of that nature. But as suddenly as a plunge into icy water, I was fully aware of where I was and what I was doing, of the throbbing of the shallow slice across my wrist, and I was terrified.

I fumbled for my handkerchief, my hands shaking so badly I could barely grasp it; it took me four tries to get it wrapped around my bleeding wrist. Standing up was even harder, and I might not have succeeded if I had not been nearly insane with desperation to escape this bitter, deadly little room.

The crying had stopped; I wondered with a nauseous compound of anger and fright if it had ever been objectively audible at all, or if I had imagined it in that strange waking dream.

I fell against the doorframe hard enough to bruise my shoulder, then lurched out into the hallway. The house was dark and cold and wrathful. The silence was worse than the crying had been; it was too much like the silence of a stalking predator. I cringed every time the floorboards creaked beneath my feet; when I reached my room, I realized I had been holding my breath. It was foolish to imagine I was safer in here than I had been in the hallway, since it was the house itself I feared, but the bland inanity of the guest room seemed less threatening than those neglected rooms on the third floor.

I sat down on the bed and unwrapped the bloodstained handkerchief from around my wrist. The bleeding had stopped, but despite my reluctance to leave this room, the cut clearly needed to be washed out and disinfected. Grimly, I got the mercurochrome out of my kit and headed to the bathroom before I could talk myself out of it.

As I was putting the cap back on the mercurochrome bottle, the cut disinfected and bandaged to the best of my ability, the crying started again. Luckily, my fingers tightened around the bottle rather than releasing it, thus sparing me from explaining to Mr Oleander why the bathroom had been erratically painted mercurochrome orange. I put the bottle down with the exaggerated care of a drunk and closed it firmly. I realized I was muttering, almost chanting, "I'm not listening to you," and forced myself to stop. It was not helping.

I took my supplies back to my bedroom. I closed and locked the door. And then I opened the curtains and dragged a chair over to the window and waited for the sun to rise over Thirdhop Scarp.

V

On Monday morning, I was waiting for Dr Starkweather when he arrived at the museum.

He checked quite visibly on the threshold of the main office, and I was bitterly amused at the wariness with which he said, "Good morning, Mr Booth."

"Good morning," I said. I did not want to have this conversation in front of the politely avid Miss Tilley, although she would inevitably hear it if Dr Starkweather lost his temper. I was hoping he would not, but I did not delude myself. He was not going to appreciate my errand.

Dr Starkweather was an autocrat, but not a fool; he sized up the situation and said, "Miss Tilley, tell Mr Hornsby that I'll see him after I've spoken to Mr Booth. Come in, Mr Booth."

I followed Dr Starkweather into his office and carefully closed the door behind me. Dr Starkweather circled around his desk and sat down. I heard him sigh, although I did not think he intended me to. "What can I do for you, Mr Booth?"

I had rehearsed my arguments half the night, but they all deserted me, and I blurted, "I can't go back to Thirdhop Scarp."

"*Can't?*" said Dr Starkweather, his eyebrows rising. "Why not?"

I opened my mouth and closed it again. I could not tell Dr Starkweather that the house had tried to make me kill myself. I said, "I'm never going to be able to, er, convince Miss Parrington to distrust Marcus Oleander. And..." I clutched desperately for something that would sound convincing and sane. "I'm falling more and more behind in my work."

"Yes," said Dr Starkweather. "I know."

I flinched and lost the last shreds of my composure. "I would rather resign," I said.

Dr Starkweather sat and looked at me. I swallowed hard, but I did not let my chin drop, and although I could not hold his gaze, I forced myself to keep looking back each time I looked away.

The silence deepened, thickened. I had never defied Dr Starkweather to his face before; in general, I did my best not to remind him I existed. He had threatened to fire me on occasion, but I had never threatened to resign.

Dr Starkweather's expression was that of a man discovering a bomb in his desk drawer. He said cautiously, not quite making it a question, "We should be very sorry to lose you."

"I should be very sorry to go," I said. "But I *cannot...*" My voice cracked, and I did not try to complete my sentence.

"And I admit," Dr Starkweather said, like a man prodding the bomb in his desk drawer with a pencil, "there does not seem to be any *particular* point to the museum's indefinitely continuing to lose your services every Friday."

"Any of the junior curators would be able to finish the, er, catalogue if Mr Oleander desired it," I said. I doubted anyone else would be as vulnerable to Thirdhop Scarp as I was, and I was very close to not caring if they were. Rank, craven selfishness on my part, and I did not care about that, either.

"Hmmph," said Dr Starkweather, and I knew he was considering which of the junior curators he was most irritated by.

"Perhaps they might be better at… that is, they might have better luck with Miss Parrington as well," I said.

Dr Starkweather scowled at me. "Have you actually *spoken* to Miss Parrington?"

"Er," I said. "I… that is, it has been difficult to know what tack—"

"Mr Booth. Yes or no?"

"…No."

Dr Starkweather swelled like a bullfrog, his face purpling, and I thought Miss Tilley was going to have her curiosity satisfied, but then he exhaled loudly and deflated again. "Mr Booth," he said, "surely you can see that this will not do."

"She will tell Mr Oleander whatever I say to her. Unless I convince her, which I don't think I can."

"Then you will have a perfect excuse for not returning to Thirdhop Scarp," Dr Starkweather said. "*And* you will have alienated Miss Parrington, which surely you will find a consummation devoutly to be wished."

"But I thought I was supposed *not* to alienate Miss Parrington?" I said in bewilderment.

"Mr Booth, do you deliberately seek out ways to make my life more difficult?"

"No," I said, still bewildered.

Dr Starkweather rubbed his forehead with his thick fingers. "If you speak to Miss Parrington, even if you fail, I will be able to tell Mrs Crowe that you tried. It will not make her *happy*, precisely, but it will make her less *unhappy* than if you make no effort at all, and that in turn will make it possible for me to persuade her that you are not to blame and thus should not be penalized."

He raised his eyebrows at me, and this time I thought I understood. "Ah," I said. "You mean I have to go back."

"That would be the short version," agreed Dr Starkweather.

I WAS NEXT to useless all that week, rehearsing—both awake and asleep—what I would say to Miss Parrington. Even knowing how little good it had done me to rehearse my conversation with Dr Starkweather, I could not keep my mind from running on the same exhausted track. On Thursday, Mr Lucent asked me irritably if I had been pithed.

On Friday, I boarded the Pittmanville train again, praying that it would be for the last time. The trip—with perverse cruelty—seemed to be over as soon as begun.

I found when I disembarked that I would be sharing Mr Oleander's automobile with Myra Blackburn, a prospect that nearly made me turn on my heel and board the train again.

"Mr Booth!" she said, as if she were both delighted and surprised. She might indeed have been delighted, unlikely though that seemed, but I realized uneasily that she was not in the slightest surprised. She did not make the mistake of trying to flirt with me, merely said, "The car will be back in a few minutes. There are some errands Marcus wants to have done, and I said I'd wait for you so you wouldn't worry you'd been forgotten."

"Very kind," I said feebly.

I do not know how she did it, for I am no conversationalist at the best of times and I was wary of her nearly to the point of mutism, but by the time the chauffeur pulled the car up in front of the station, I was describing the Parrington's holdings of American esoterica to her, and she had just asked an intelligent question about the correspondence of the occultist John Harmon Peabody. The chauffeur held the door expressionlessly, and I climbed in beside Myra Blackburn.

She did not try to sit too close. She continued the conversation about John Harmon Peabody and his letter-writing until we had left the town behind, and then, after a short, perfectly innocuous silence, said, "I can't help noticing, Mr Booth, that you have a remarkable effect on the house at Thirdhop Scarp."

"I beg your pardon," I said, an answer so inadequate that Mrs Blackburn laughed out loud.

"Oh, no," she said, and her tone might have sounded friendly if I had not been able to see her eyes. "You know exactly what I mean. It took me an embarrassingly long time to realize it, but that's your own fault for being so self-effacing. I should," she added, mostly to herself, "have paid more attention to Alexis. He's been fascinated since the first time he saw you."

"I… er…" She could have found no surer way to horrify me if she had asked.

"The house *responds* to you, Mr Booth," Mrs

Blackburn proceeded, leaning forward a little even as I shrank back. "And that's why I need your help."

"My... help?" It was not, somehow, the word I had been expecting.

"We need to find a way to quiet the house," she said. "The poltergeist activity, in particular—it's become too destructive. We've been trying all week, but we can't get through."

As if she were talking about a downed telephone line.

There were a number of things another man might have said, perhaps a reference to sleeping dogs and why it was better to let them lie, or acidly pointing out that the Order Aurorae Aeternae had gotten exactly what they wanted.

I had to try three times before I could get any words out at all. "And you think I'm going to..."

Make any difference? I would have finished, but Mrs Blackburn either interpreted my question as defiance or chose to, for she said with a glittering smile, "Oh, I'm quite sure of it. Or I can always tell Griselda Parrington the real reason you're here."

The expression on my face made her laugh. "It's hardly a secret, Mr Booth. Griselda is probably the only person in the house who *hasn't* guessed. But I don't think she'll be very pleased when she learns, do you?"

No, I was fairly sure Miss Parrington would feel that I had betrayed her—and that led in a remarkably straight line to the end of my tenure at the Parrington Museum. Neither Mrs Crowe nor Dr Starkweather was likely to defend me for making such a botch of my commission.

The look I gave Mrs Blackburn was undoubtedly surly, but she read my capitulation in it and said, "Splendid. We convene after dinner—just don't try to vanish the way you usually do." She had too much elegance to repeat her threat. She knew she did not need to.

Of course, if I could persuade Miss Parrington to leave Thirdhop Scarp, I need neither go through with Mrs Blackburn's séance nor fear being denounced. And I would never have to spend another night—another hour—another *second*—in Thirdhop Scarp. I would pay for a room at the decaying Pittmanville Hotel out of my own pocket, even if I had to sleep on the floor and leave the bed for the rats and centipedes. It would be worth it, and I knew that with every wretched atom of my being as soon as I walked through Thirdhop Scarp's ornate front doors.

The house's inchoate, seeking anger welled up to meet me, unassuaged by whatever measures had been attempted during the week. It was like walking into a swarm of blind bees. I could feel the hairs on my forearms rising with the wildness crackling through Thirdhop Scarp, but the house still could not find me, could not find any of the strange, vile, scuttling creatures that taunted it with their squeakings and scratchings...

I shook my head in a sharp jerk, clearing it of the house's angry, buzzing whispers.

"Are you all right, Mr Booth?" said Mrs Blackburn with a sort of smug concern that made me long for the courage to slap her.

"Fine," I said, and Marcus Oleander made his entrance, surrounded by his fawning court. In the excitement, it was easy to slip away.

* * *

I SPENT THE afternoon vacillating between trying futilely to work and trying futilely to find Miss Parrington. I could not concentrate well enough to do any of the more complicated tasks that lay before me, and even when I tried to find simpler things for myself to do, as one does with an eager but inept assistant, I would think of another place to look for Miss Parrington and go haring off without completing the job on which I had been working—a habit that I loathe. And then I would come back, having failed to find Miss Parrington again, and be unable to remember what I had been doing. Finally, I set myself to combing the shelves for duplicates, and it was while engaged on this task that I pulled out a volume of the *Opera* of the Spanish mystic Fernando Villareal y Garza and found a row of books double-stacked behind. I promptly sat down, stacked Villareal's nine volume *Opera* beside me and stared at my discovery: a row of pedestrian decaying books—Thomas Paine, Thomas Jefferson, a privately printed *History of Pittman County* from 1843, the novels of Nathaniel Hawthorne. I pulled out *The House of the Seven Gables* and checked the flyleaf—where iron-gall ink turning rusty with age said with a flourish, *Leonard Tull*.

I admit that I sat there in bafflement for some time. T. Zacharias Tull had hidden his father's books—for no other shelf in the library was double-stacked like this, and he must have deliberately chosen the Villareal for its oddly sized volumes. He had hidden them, as if they were shameful, but he had not gotten rid of them. Sentiment seemed grossly out of character, and the books certainly were not valuable for any other reason. Finally, I replaced *The House of the Seven Gables*, reshelved the Villareal, and went to look for Miss Parrington again.

She was not in any of the public rooms of the house; she was either not in her bedroom or refusing to answer my knock. I could neither believe she had gone up to the third floor nor bring myself to go look. I had made forays into the gardens and failed to find her among the roses or on the croquet green or under the elaborate lattices of the grape arbor. I did steel myself to check the ornamental lake, but there was no sign of her there—not that I had any clear idea of what I would have done if I had come upon her sinking beneath the lake's turbid surface.

I returned to the house in a welter of depression and dread. Each time I entered the house, I felt its hatred more jarringly, and it was really only to put off the inevitable for a few more moments that I followed the path around to the west side of the house and the view over the escarpment.

The house gave the impression of being built on the very lip of the cliff, but that was not actually true. It was, however, built much closer to the edge than I thought comfortable, never mind safe, and the gravel path was separated only by a strip of dense evergreen shrub from the iron fence that was the last defense against accidents—of either the accidental or deliberate variety. The fence looked very flimsy to me, and I kept carefully to the inner curve of the path.

The house jutted out at the join of the north and main wings—one of the servants' stairs, I thought, although I had not a confident enough grasp of the house's geography to say whether it was the one Randolph Tull had fallen down. I came around the corner and was startled to discover a bench tucked into the odd blind angle, even more startled to discover sitting on it Griselda

Parrington and Christabel Hallett, heads together in what was clearly an intense discussion.

I pulled up short. They both jerked stiffly upright; before she recognized me, there was a moment of wild near-panic on Mrs Hallett's face that told me as plainly as words that she had been fomenting rebellion against Marcus Oleander.

"Oh, Mr Booth!" said Miss Parrington. "How you startled me!"

I mumbled an apology and then stood awkwardly. I had nerved myself to talk to Miss Parrington, although my nerve had been eroding throughout the afternoon, but it was not a discussion I wanted to have in front of witnesses, and particularly not the fanatical and power-hungry Mrs Hallett. On the other hand, the shadows were already lengthening toward dusk, and I was running out of time.

"Did you need something, Mr Booth?" prompted Mrs Hallett. It was not a subtle hint, and I knew that I should take it, that nothing about this situation was going to encourage Miss Parrington to listen to me, but I was desperate, and I stood my ground.

"Did you need to speak to *me*, Mr Booth?" Miss Parrington said, sounding both hopeful and surprised.

"Just for a moment," I said and took a step toward the fence.

"Oh, Christabel won't mind. Just for a moment, Christabel!" Miss Parrington stood and followed me over as close to the fence as the shrubbery allowed; I wished, tiredly, that Griselda Parrington could do anything without *fluttering*.

And then she was standing next to me, closer than was either necessary or desirable, looking up into my face.

Stepping away from her would mean falling into the hedge; I swallowed hard and said, "Miss Parrington, I... er... I think you should leave."

"I beg your pardon?" she said, bewildered rather than angry, although my phrasing had been so maladroit that anger would have been quite justified.

"Leave Thirdhop Scarp, I mean!" I said hastily. "It... er... it isn't safe."

"Why, whatever do you mean, Mr Booth?" She turned to appeal to her companion. "Christabel, Mr Booth says Thirdhop Scarp isn't safe."

I was raised from earliest childhood in the belief that a gentleman never stoops to obscenity or profanity—*and whatever else you may be*, my father had said dryly, *you will be a gentleman*. Thus, I did not curse them both as Christabel Hallett stood and crossed the path to join us. I also did not fling myself over the iron fence, although the temptation was nearly as strong.

"Isn't safe *how*, Mr Booth?" said Mrs Hallett. She was square-jawed for a woman, with broad cheekbones and gray exophthalmic eyes; she looked a little like a pug, and I found her face almost impossible to read. Was she genuinely concerned? Curious? Or was she merely waiting for me to supply the ammunition for mockery?

Regardless, I was already committed to this conversation. I could not now say *oh never mind* and leave, if for no other reason than that I knew Miss Parrington would follow me. And whatever their motives, they were both waiting for me to speak. If I could persuade *both* of them to leave (and Conrad Hallett, following wherever his wife led), maybe the disaster I felt louring over Thirdhop Scarp could be averted. I said, "...Don't you feel it? How angry the house is?"

"*Angry?*" said Mrs Hallett, as one who had never heard the word before in her life.

"The stones," I said. "The broken china."

"The spirits struggle to communicate with us," said Mrs Hallett. "Lacking voices, they use what means they have." I was morally certain she was quoting someone, although it was a toss-up whether it was Mr Oleander or Mrs Blackburn. Beside her, Miss Parrington nodded earnestly.

They did not feel the house's vicious anger. They *could* not, if they were echoing platitudes about communication. I floundered, hamstrung by my own incredulity. How could they not feel how much Thirdhop Scarp hated them?

I could not tell them about Agnes Tull's study and the waiting knife. I could not tell them about Cecilia. Everything else was an olio of speculation and hearsay and rank, arrant gossip. I said, a last resort, "Do you not dream about being suffocated in the dark?"

"Your dreams say more about you than they do about the house, Mr Booth," Mrs Hallett said primly.

"I'm sorry you are unhappy here," Miss Parrington said, putting her hand on my forearm. "I'll tell Blanche she should send someone else."

Which would only convince Mrs Crowe and Dr Starkweather that I had failed—worse than failed, that I had purposely sabotaged the mission they had given me in order to escape the necessity of completing it. "That isn't... er, that is, you needn't," I said, stepping awkwardly sideways to get away from her hand. "Honestly, I..." It would have been untrue to say I was not worried about myself. I settled on, "Please consider the possibility that I'm right."

"How can you be right when you speak from fear?" Mrs Hallett said, which was some of the most reasonable-sounding and unanswerable nonsense I had ever encountered. "The spirits mean us no harm, Mr Booth, and we must be open to their messages in order to hear them. Please do not make that task harder by encouraging fear and hatred."

She had no idea what she was talking about, but sincerity rang in every foolish word. Even if I still found her face unreadable, I could not feel any conviction in the idea that she was attempting charlatanry along the lines of Mr Oleander. She truly believed there was no malevolence at work in Thirdhop Scarp.

Miss Parrington said, "Really, Mr Booth, you should attend dear Alexis's séances. Then you would understand better."

"Yes," said Mrs Hallett. "I agree that the *phenomena* can be upsetting, if one does not know that they are only the result of frustration. When you have spoken to the spirits, Mr Booth, you will cease to fear them."

I doubted that proposition most profoundly, but Miss Parrington was already chiming in agreement: "There's no *malice*, Mr Booth. They're just lost and need someone to listen."

If she did not recognize murderous rage when she witnessed it, then I had no hope of swaying her. I sighed and—as it was the best way of disentangling myself from the coils of their fervent desire to convert me—confessed, "I will be at the séance tonight."

"Splendid!" said Mrs Hallett, clearly pleased with this evidence of her own rhetorical powers.

"Oh, that *will* be lovely," said Miss Parrington, and there was not the faintest wisp of irony in her anywhere.

*   *   *

THE SÉANCE THAT evening followed a dinner that was like something Dante forgot to put in the *Inferno*. Mrs Hallett was continuing to sow sedition; although she had not yet reached the point of challenging Oleander outright, it was only a matter of time before she would. Those guests who were not listening thoughtfully to her were watching in frank fascination the skirmishing between Michael Kitchener and Myra Blackburn—which Marcus Oleander was now making no attempt to stop or even mediate. I was seated halfway down the table, in a position where I could hear both conversations at once and thus could hear neither completely. But the atmosphere was poisonous, and I longed to be able to escape—to the library, to my bedroom, to the Pittmanville Hotel. My office at the museum seemed as unobtainable as Cockaigne.

My torment was at least not drawn out by any lingering over coffee. Everyone was palpably eager to begin the séance, and I misliked the avid way they watched Alexis. Behind his elegant and dark façade, he looked tired, and I caught the barest flicker of a resentful glance at Mrs Blackburn when she put her hand on his arm and announced that it was time for the séance to begin.

This time, I was as far away from Alexis as Mrs Blackburn could maneuver me. She sat next to me herself, her hand soft and cold in mine. On the other side, I was trapped by the hairy grip of her husband. They wanted to make very sure of me, a realization which sat like a lead ingot in the pit of my stomach, and the fact that I had my back to the fireplace made everything just that much worse. My shoulders were already tensing in expectation of Emily Tull's ghostly fire.

Alexis flashed a smile around the circle as Marcus Oleander finished lighting the candles and took his place. "I can feel that the spirits are very anxious to speak tonight."

"They are beginning to know us," Mrs Blackburn said. "They know they can trust us to listen."

They know they can trust us to be taken in, I did not say. I kept my gaze fixed on the tabletop through the rodomontade of blessings and invocations, did not look up even when Alexis invited the spirits to speak and at last fell silent. I was miserably aware that my hands were sweating. I looked up once; across the table from me, Mrs Seftick had her eyes closed, her head thrown back, an expression on her face of intense concentration. I looked down again quickly, embarrassed for reasons I could not fully explain.

There were snatches of the Cathcart children all evening—a girl dreamily reciting the names of the roses in the garden; another girl and the boy, Constance and John Aloysius, Jr., who gave their names freely and demanded ours in return; the youngest Cathcart child, Louisa, would only ask anxiously for her mother, but Helen Cathcart was never there to answer.

We had a strange, circling conversation with Laura Dunaphy, murdered in passing by J. A. Cathcart, in which it became clear that even though she had not died within the house, she was still trapped by it. She kept asking how much farther she had to go. Everyone else assumed she meant in order to find help; I knew she meant in order to escape. But escape was no more possible for her than it was for the dreadful thing in the lake. They were both bound to the house.

Mostly, that evening, the Order Aurorae Aeternae

spoke to two housemaids who had died sometime before the turn of the century. The first, whose name was Minnie Slocum, had died in childbirth of a child whose existence she had hidden right up to the moment the too-heavy bleeding started. The child had died with her—we could hear its weak mewling from time to time—but Minnie was preoccupied, to the almost complete exclusion of other concerns, with a mortal terror of Zenobia Webster Tull. That terror was why she had hidden her pregnancy—not because she would have been dismissed without a character reference, although she almost certainly would have been—but because she could not face Mrs Tull. I thought that same terror, unameliorated by death or the passing decades, was the reason she would not name her child's father, which made it likely bordering on inevitable that the father was Randolph Tull (or, as an outside possibility, T. Zacharias, although it seemed a rather plebeian sin for his tastes) and the dead child a cousin of Christabel Hallett. I was grateful that Mrs Hallett did not seem to have realized that herself.

The other housemaid was named Bridget Mahoney. She, like Randolph Tull, had died of a fall down the stairs; she was certain that she had been pushed. Mrs Seftick and Mrs Hallett asked questions about who would have wanted to hurt her and who could have been behind her in that narrow third floor hall. Bridget Mahoney insisted the answer in each case was *no one*, and yet she would not be swayed from her conviction that she had been pushed. Finally, Miss Quincey asked, "Who do you think pushed you, Bridget?" and Bridget Mahoney, in a hoarse, confiding whisper, said, "I think the house did it."

Like a submerged rock ripping the keel out of a ship, that answer broke up the séance. No one wanted to believe she was telling the simple, literal truth, and efforts to get her to admit that she had tripped, or that she was using some kind of metaphor for someone she did not want to name, merely drove her into a sullen, baffled silence. I wanted to tell her that I believed her, but I did not have the courage. Very shortly thereafter, Alexis said, "This room is clear of the unseen," and the séance was over.

The Order Aurorae Aeternae stood up and milled around. I heard fragments of conversation, mostly theories of how Bridget Mahoney had died. "She was probably drunk," a man said sourly behind my chair, but when I tried to twist to see who it was, Captain Blackburn's hand caught mine again, pinching the bones.

"You don't want to go anywhere yet, Mr Booth," the captain said, in a voice pitched just to carry to my ears.

"But," I said, glancing involuntarily at the elegant gray and scarlet back of Myra Blackburn. "She said…"

The captain snorted. "This wasn't the *real* séance. This was just window dressing for the punters. Once Oleander gets rid of them, we'll get down to business."

Now at least I knew where Alexis had picked up the word "punters"—and possibly also where he had picked up that breezy contempt for them, so different from Mrs Blackburn's delicate, watchful poise. I had dismissed Captain Blackburn as merely his wife's shadow, but perhaps that was an addition to my dismally long list of mistakes.

If I tried to pull away from him, I would fail, and the best outcome I could see was being humiliated in front of Marcus Oleander and all his guests. Certainly, none of them would come to my rescue, and the captain's hard grip suggested that I would pay for any trouble I caused.

I sat still and waited, watching the crowd disperse. The Sefticks, it turned out, were punters. So were the Halletts and Miss Quincey. As for Miss Parrington, I could think of no better word to describe her, and I was not surprised to see Oleander chivvying her gently out of the room. He was careful not to close the door until she was out of earshot. There were now seven remaining: Marcus Oleander, Captain and Mrs Blackburn, Mr Bell, Mr Kitchener, Alexis, and—reluctantly—myself.

The company sat down; I was once again trapped between Mrs Blackburn and the captain. "Now," Mrs Blackburn said, resuming her soft, cold violation of my hand. "Let us see if Mr Booth is indeed the key to this very stubborn door."

But there is no door, I thought, and then had no idea where the thought had come from.

"We need you to go deeper, Alexis," Marcus Oleander said, and even Alexis, who had told me Oleander was a fraud, could not help responding.

"I'm doing the best I can," he said fretfully. "It's not like using a telephone, you know."

"Of course you are," Oleander said, a fraction too warmly for sincerity.

"I don't know why you think it's going to be any different with seven," Alexis said, although I noticed he was talking to Mrs Blackburn, not to Oleander. "I can already tell you Bridget Mahoney is gone."

"It isn't Bridget Mahoney we want," said Mrs Blackburn. "Just a moment—trade places with me, darling. Perhaps it was the skin-to-skin contact with Mr Booth that improved your performance so dramatically."

Alexis looked momentarily as alarmed as I felt, but he obeyed Mrs Blackburn without a murmur. He took my hand in a light grip, barely curling his fingers. He was very carefully not looking at me, so that I could only wonder if he knew that Mrs Blackburn had blackmailed me into attending, that Captain Blackburn's painful grip was the only thing that kept me from leaving, blackmail or no.

The rest of the circle joined hands, and Alexis began his invocation. Because he was next to me, I could feel how tense he was; I heard nothing of it in his voice. I remembered that Mrs Blackburn had said they had been trying all week to "get through," and it occurred to me—distantly, but with an odd sense of having come upon something important—that Alexis Rigby was not accustomed to failure.

He finished his ritual of clichés, and there was a tense silence that stretched out minute after minute, until I began to wonder whether we would sit here like statues until dawn. I do not know how long it was before I heard someone humming. At first I thought it was someone in the circle, but realized a split-second later how ridiculous that idea was. The voice was high-pitched and wandering rather through the melody, but I recognized the tune.

"Excellent," said Mrs Blackburn, and then louder, "Hello, Emily. Will you speak to us?"

The humming stopped. We all, I think, were holding our breaths. And then that high, thin voice said wistfully, "Pretty lady."

"Thank you, Emily," Mrs Blackburn said.

"The other ladies are sleeping," Emily said. "So's one of the gentlemen. The other gentleman's writing a letter. It's a sad letter. That's why he waited until the blonde lady was asleep." Georgiana Seftick was the only blonde lady in the house.

"Why is he sad?" Mr Kitchener asked, greedy as always for gossip.

"His friend is going away, across the sea. On a boat."

But this was all standard Spiritualist fare, the sort of thing Alexis had meant when he talked about having lots of activity for the punters, and I was not surprised when Mrs Blackburn said, "Emily, is there anyone here with you?"

"All alone," Emily said and began to sing-song: "All alone, all alone." I thought, *A child* and *a madwoman*, and shivered. Captain Blackburn tightened his grip warningly.

"Emily," said Mrs Blackburn, "let us talk to your brother." Alexis had told me that Mrs Blackburn had said she was not interested in T. Zacharias Tull. I wondered if that had simply been untrue or if something had changed her mind.

"You can talk to Randolph," Emily said, although she sounded doubtful. "He never says much."

"Emily!" There was a real snap in Mrs Blackburn's voice, a week's worth of frustration shading into anger. "I want to speak to your older brother, Terence Zacharias Tull."

Emily was silent.

Later, I tried to pinpoint exactly when things began to go wrong, and my belief is that it was that moment, when Mrs Blackburn said that name. I believe that name, in that context, attracted the attention of something that had been seeking, blindly, for weeks.

It was not blind any longer.

"Emily?" said Mrs Blackburn. "Can we speak to Terence?"

In the fireplace behind me, the ghostly fire flared up.

It made a strange, faint noise, as if the chimney sobbed once, and I could see its pale light on my imprisoned hands. Emily said nothing, but I could feel that she was still there, as distinctly as if it were her hand in mine instead of Alexis's.

Patterson Bell said uneasily, "Mrs Blackburn, surely it is unwise to insist that the spirits speak if they do not want to."

Mrs Blackburn ignored him. "Is Terence here, Emily?"

"I didn't think he was," said Emily. "I thought it was safe."

"Safe?" said Mr Bell.

Mrs Blackburn said, "If Terence is here, Emily, we—"

"I thought he'd gone with Mother," said Emily. "He always did. I didn't know he was in here."

The ghost of the fire that had killed Emily Tull was radiating cold instead of heat.

"What happened, Emily?" asked Mr Bell, and I remembered that no one else knew T. Zacharias Tull had murdered his sister. The truth, once I knew it, had seemed self-evident, as if anyone walking into Thirdhop Scarp ought to be able to read it in the pattern of the wallpaper. But of course that was a fallacy; no one else *could* know the truth, because I had not told them.

"He was reading," said Emily. "He put his book down, and he said he had something to show me. I wanted to go away, but he said it was important. He said it was a gift for Mother. So I went to look, and he pushed me."

Alexis's hand jerked in mine.

"He pushed you?" Mr Bell said, as if he did not understand.

"Into the fire," said Emily.

"Your *brother* pushed you?" said Mr Kitchener.

"He always hated me," said Emily, "because Mother said I was special. He wanted to be more special and he couldn't. So he pushed me."

The ghostly fire was brighter behind me, and I could see Emily, little more than a silhouette of a child, standing near the door, as she must have stood before her brother called her over to the fireplace.

Mr Bell said, "It could have been an accident?" His voice rose almost plaintively to turn it into a question.

"He pushed me," Emily said. "I couldn't tell anybody before, but I can tell you. He pushed me, and he watched me burn."

For a long moment, no one spoke. No one knew what to say, and even Myra Blackburn apparently recognized that asking Emily to help us talk to her murderer was beyond the pale. Or perhaps she only knew that Patterson Bell would find it so, and Patterson Bell was too wealthy to offend.

No one spoke, and although Captain Blackburn's grip on my hand remained steadily just-this-side of painful, I realized that Alexis was shivering, his fingers flexing in minute twitches.

"Alexis?" I whispered, thinking vaguely that this might be an excuse to end the séance now, before anything worse happened, if Alexis was becoming ill.

Alexis shuddered violently, his head snapping back and his hand spasming shut on mine. I yelped, and Mr Kitchener started to say something, probably about unnecessary and distracting noise, but he was interrupted and drowned out by a great, hollow knocking that seemed to come from everywhere at once. If I could have freed either of my hands, I would have done it, but I could not. Alexis and Captain Blackburn were like twin manacles, and the more I tugged, the tighter they gripped.

Alexis's head came down, and he looked around the circle. When he turned toward me, I saw that his eyes were closed, but the impression of *looking* was horribly strong, and I twisted my head away.

"Strangers," said a voice, and although Alexis's mouth was moving, it was not his voice: the pitch was too high and the accent nothing like Alexis's careful prep school vowels. But beyond that, the voice simply did not belong to Alexis Rigby. Even as gifted an actor as I suspected him to be, he could not have produced that voice. It was the voice of someone else. "Strangers in my house."

We were all frozen in place. I thought wildly of poor Bridget Mahoney, who knew the house had killed her although she could not explain how. This cold malevolence, rolling like a fog bank through the room, must have been what she felt in the moment before her death, just as I had felt it when I blundered out of Agnes Tull's study. I had been lucky, Bridget Mahoney unlucky. Somehow, the house had found her, just at the top of those steep servant's stairs. All it needed, as it had proved with its apports and knocking and other manifestations, was to be able to find a target.

And now it had found us.

It was Michael Kitchener who spoke to it, either out of insane courage or an inability to understand the danger. He said, "Who are you?" and the thing in Alexis laughed, a harsh cracked sound that gripped Alexis like a seizure.

"I am no one," it said. "I am a prison, built to hold thin air. I am the weight of eighty years of death." It turned suddenly to me, so that I flinched back as from a striking cobra, and said, "I am your nightmares."

"You talk as if you weren't a person," Mr Kitchener said.

"I'm not," it said and laughed again.

"Oh, come now!" said Mr Kitchener, rushing blindly into the darkness. "You know that's not true."

The thing was silent, and my sense of danger increased. Mr Kitchener had unwittingly said something that threatened this visitor, and the only way he could have done that was if he had, however accidentally, spoken the truth.

"I am no one," it said again, harshly, "but I know who *you* are. You steal money from your master, Michael Kitchener, secure in the knowledge that he has stolen so much that he will never notice. You steal, and then you spend what you have stolen on shabby imitations of the things you desire. And this is why you will never be more than a shabby imitation of your master."

Even in the dim light of the candles, Mr Kitchener's color was ghastly, his mouth drawn in a painful rictus that was only the most grotesque approximation of a smile— and that, I thought, was automatic, not anything over which he had conscious control. If he had fainted, I would not have been surprised.

But he did not; he even rallied, managing to say, "That's... a lie," although given how breathless and uneven his voice was, he would have done better to stay silent. He could not have imagined any of us would believe him.

"Is it?" said the thing using Alexis Rigby's mouth. "Is it indeed?"

"Madam," said Patterson Bell, and I wondered how he had decided it was female, "this behavior is—"

"Mr Bell," it said. "You want to know what happened to your son, don't you? I can tell you."

It paused, but Patterson Bell failed to speak, failed to deny what was, after all, the truth, and it said, audibly gloating: "He died screaming, Mr Bell, trapped in the wreckage of his burning airplane. His crew could have saved him, but they all hated him so much, with his bullying and his petty cruelty and his lies, that they just left him there."

"You are a liar," Patterson Bell said, with great dignity, but I could hear the first terrible cracks of doubt in his voice.

"Am I? But each of those men will have to live for the rest of his life with the knowledge that he hated a man enough to let him burn to death without lifting a finger to save him, and that man was your son. You knew they were lying, Mr Bell. Why else have you spent all this time searching for the truth?" The thing in Alexis's body smiled, the lips drawing back from the teeth like a snarling dog. "He died screaming for *you*."

Patterson Bell was silent, as ashen-faced as Michael Kitchener; I tried again to free my hands and break the circle, but I could not. Despite the devastation this visitor was wreaking, despite the fact that it had, as best I could tell, *possessed* Alexis, no one else seemed to have any sense of danger.

Or perhaps they were mesmerized, like rabbits in a field crouched beneath the shadow of a hawk.

Alexis's face, eyes still closed, turned toward Myra Blackburn—it was going around the circle, person by person, in a parody of fairness. "Dearest Myra!" it said. "Or should I say, Mary Jane?"

For a moment, it was as if Myra Blackburn's face simply collapsed. For a moment, there was no force, no poise. For a moment, Myra Blackburn was ugly. "Who are you?" she said, and her voice was as cracked and warbled as her face. "Zacharias? But I never…"

"I told you. I am no one." It laughed again. "I am Legion. And I know everything about you, Mary Jane Herzog."

"You can't," she said. "You *can't*."

"Shall I prove it?" This time it did not pause. "You left your parents' farm without a backwards glance when you were seventeen, although your mother was dying and your five younger siblings would soon have no one to care for them. You persuaded T. Zacharias Tull to teach you by seducing him, although he was some thirty years your senior, and when you had extracted every last scrap of knowledge you could from him, you left *him* without a backwards glance. You stay with your current husband—whose name is no more Blackburn than yours is—because you find him useful. He would die for you, and you would let him. You use your little protégé's talents as a screen for your own practices, since all the gullible fools who want to speak to the dead would be horrified to discover that you were actually practicing necromancy. Shall I tell them of your successes, Mary Jane Herzog?"

Marcus Oleander said, "Spirit of the darkness, I abjure thee. Spirit of the darkness—"

"I see you, Charles Marsh," said the thing in Alexis, in its old, rusted, not quite human voice. "I see you prancing around my house, bedding your women, lording it over those fool enough to believe your pretty lies. But who's the fool, Charles Marsh? Who's believed every word this woman told you?"

If Oleander had had the simple fixity of purpose to continue his banishment, he might have succeeded. But

103

he fell into the trap just as the others had. "What do you mean?"

"She's a liar, Charles Marsh," the voice said, almost crooned. "She told you what you wanted to hear, and you did not question her. You didn't even *wonder* what it was she might really be after."

"For God's sake, who *are* you?" Mrs Blackburn cried hoarsely.

There was a pause, and the voice said, as if coming suddenly to a decision, "I don't want you in my house, Charles Marsh. You *or* that brazen Jezebel with her tin soldier. Get out."

"But—"

"Get out, get out, get out!" The voice rose into a shriek like a November gale, and the gale was there, too, battering at my face, stabbing through my clothes, malice made palpable, rage given force.

If I screamed, I could not hear myself.

The circle finally broke. Emily's ghostly fire vanished, the candles were snuffed as one, and the electric lights flared and went out with a distinct pop. My hands were suddenly released, and I shoved back so violently that my chair fell over; mine was not the only one. There were several minutes of confusion; someone's foot struck me with enough force to leave me breathless; everyone seemed to be shouting. Finally someone, who turned out to be Patterson Bell, found both a candle and a match and restored, if not order, at least light.

I sat up warily as Patterson Bell moved around the room, lighting the candles in their elaborate and hideous candelabra. He stopped by the door and tried the light switch; nothing happened, and I did not think he had expected anything to.

Alexis was sitting on the floor by the fireplace, looking dazed and ill. Michael Kitchener was standing in the middle of the room, staring at the wide-open door in confusion. Captain Blackburn was leaning anxiously over his wife, who looked nearly as ill as Alexis; her hair, which she wore in an old-fashioned chignon, had half come down—it was as near to ludicrous as I could ever imagine her appearing.

Of Marcus Oleander there was no sign.

Patterson Bell came back to the table, righting a chair and sitting down. I noticed that he did not even glance at Mrs Blackburn—and he, like I, had been raised a gentleman. Necromancy put Myra Blackburn beyond the pale of even a seeker after knowledge such as Patterson Bell. But, then, he had found the knowledge he sought, and his profit was ashes and bitter wormwood. I could see the struggle in his face, and I said, "You do not know that it told the truth."

He shook his head. "No, I am afraid that—"

The clamor I had been aware of outside the drawing room suddenly increased. The Order Aurorae Aeternae had found us.

They surged into the room, all talking at once so that I could catch only fragments about knocking and a sort of roaring sound and "the parlor is ruined," and then Christabel Hallett's voice cut through the din, complaining, "and the front door is wide open. I thought Marcus told them to be sure—"

"Marcus!" gasped Michael Kitchener, so like the heroine in a melodrama that it would have been absurd except for the fact that he was not acting—for once, Michael Kitchener did not have one eye slyly on his audience. He bolted out of the room, and I realized—crucial, culpable seconds too late—that he was heading out into the darkness to look for his fled master.

"Stop him!" I cried, floundering to my feet, but by the time they figured out what I meant, Michael Kitchener was gone.

And then I had to dissuade them from following him. "We'll never find him," I said again and again. "The grounds are too extensive. We have no idea which way he went." And there was something prowling the grounds that we did not want to meet, but I did not mention her. I was not sure, even now, that they would believe me, and I was afraid it might make some of them even more eager to search.

The dining room and the breakfast parlor both showed evidence of the house's anger, with chairs overturned and curtains ripped down, but it was the study—the lovingly restored, nearly sacrosanct study—that had borne the brunt of the house's fury. Every picture had been torn from the walls, and the glass was like a carpet of diamonds. Every book had been thrown out of the bookcase; the desk had been heaved over on its side, all the drawers pulled out, and the chair was so many mahogany sticks. Upholstery had been ripped and horsehair flung everywhere, along with scraps of the pictures, all of which had been ripped to shreds. The ivy trellis wallpaper was hanging from the walls in strips. I was staring at the streamers of canvas drooping from a gilt frame when I was struck by a terrible thought. I managed not to betray myself with an exclamation, and it was not difficult to slink away without anyone noticing.

I did not run to the library, but only because I did not want to draw attention. My hands were shaking when I opened the door, and I fumbled at the light switch like a drunkard. The devastation an angry poltergeist could wreak on these old, fragile books was simultaneously unimaginable and all too vivid, and I flinched when I finally managed to press the switch.

The library was untouched.

I stared uncomprehendingly even as the relief made my knees buckle, and I had to clutch for a chair. Zenobia Webster Tull's study had looked as though it had been the target of a cyclone, but nothing in here had been disturbed, not even so much as an index card.

I touched the book lying on the table (Bartholomew Stanes Harcourt's copy of the 1738 edition of *A Treatise upon the Especial Providences of the New England Colonies as Collected over These Past Three Score Years*, by the Reverend Meshach Williams) just to convince myself of its existence, and a voice said behind me, "You care much more about these books than any of the people here, don't you?"

I recognized the voice as belonging to Alexis even as I lurched to my feet, banging my hip against the table as I turned.

"I don't blame you," he continued, and I could not tell if he realized how badly he had startled me. He was disheveled, and his eyes in their dark hollows still had the lost look I had noticed in the drawing room, as if something vital inside him had been jarred out of place. "No, I don't blame you at all."

His voice cracked on the last word, and he brought his hands up slowly to cover his face. His hands were shaking as badly as mine were.

"Alexis?" I said cautiously. "Are you..."

"She told me the truth," he said, muffled behind his hands, but perfectly understandable. "She finally told me the truth."

"She" could only be Myra Blackburn—or Mary Jane Herzog, although it was all but impossible to think of her by that name—and I was now alarmed enough to approach. "Alexis?"

"I'm a useful tool," he said, and the raw bleakness of his voice told me, like a deluge of information I did not want, much more about Alexis and his relationship with his guardian than he would ever have wished me to know.

He scrubbed his hands roughly down his cheeks and said, "I knew she didn't... that is, I never believed the things she said to other people, and I knew she'd never be like *that*, not really, but I thought... I thought we were *partners*."

You thought you weren't a punter, I finished, but even when I had been Alexis's age, I could never have been cruel enough to say it aloud.

"Come sit down," I said as kindly as I could, and he obeyed the suggestion, although I was not sure he was fully aware of doing so.

He sat for a moment, staring blankly at the green shaded table lamp, and then heaved a deep, sighing breath and straightened his shoulders. "Well," he said, with a fair assumption of briskness. "It doesn't matter if Myra... what Myra thinks of me." The word *love,* though unspoken, was painfully present. "I really just came to ask you if you knew what that..." He hesitated, searching for a word (I suspected) to describe the malignant spirit that had invaded the séance, and in that silence, we both clearly heard a motor car finish making the turn around the circle in front of the house and accelerate toward the main road.

Alexis and I stared at each other. What little color he had regained drained away from his face, and he said,

"Myra," with so little force behind the syllables that it was only because I watched his lips move that I knew he had spoken at all.

"We don't... er, we don't *know* that," I said, even though I knew—as one knows things in nightmares—that he was correct. "It might be Mr Oleander. Or Mr Kitchener."

"The captain can drive," Alexis said. "Marcus can't. And if you think Michael Kitchener was in any shape to steal an automobile..."

"No, but—"

"No, it's Myra. She was desperate to get away, and the captain would die trying to move a mountain if she asked him to. He wouldn't blink at theft. He's still useful. I guess I'm not." His breathing hitched slightly, but only slightly—it was as if this final and most unequivocal betrayal had shaken him back into control of himself.

"And they've stranded us all here," I said, realizing. "Unless—did any of the guests bring their own vehicles?"

"No," Alexis said. "Marcus strongly discourages it. He likes being lord of the manor."

"So we're..." I swallowed hard. "Trapped."

"That's a rather melodramatic way of putting it, Mr Booth," Alexis said; he even sounded amused.

"*No,*" I said, sharply enough that I surprised us both. "Don't back away from it again and pretend you don't know what I'm talking about. We are trapped in this house with something..." But I had no idea how to describe it. And my silence seemed to goad Alexis as my words never had.

"So what do you propose we *do?*" he snarled. "Exorcism? Fire and salt? A cup of tea and a cookie? It's not as if there's a guidebook for this sort of thing." (Actually, there were several in this room alone, but I did not try to tell him so.) "It's not like any ghost I've ever encountered, and in fact I'm not sure it's a ghost at all!"

He stopped then, staring at me almost defiantly. "Not a ghost?" I said. "What do you mean?"

"I... I'm not sure." He had been expecting me, I thought, to tell him not to be childish or overdramatic, as he had told me Myra Blackburn did. But I was not sure that it was possible to be overdramatic about the thing that had taken over the séance.

I said slowly, "It said it wasn't anyone, but... it was, that is, I thought it was lying."

"Maybe?" Alexis was frowning, struggling to articulate something that was clearly more instinctive than rational; it was the most honest expression I had ever seen on his face. "Even if one assumed, hypothetically, that a house could speak, I don't think it would be so... *personal*. That... that presence hated Marcus in a way that I just can't imagine..." He trailed off, still frowning. "The house would have no reason to *care*."

"The house hates us all equally just because we're here," I said. "That was someone with a grudge against Mr Oleander."

"Yes, so it must be... or it must *have been* a person once. But it wasn't a ghost like the Cathcart children or Bridget Mahoney. It's still active."

I was about to say that I did not understand, when suddenly I did. "It hates Mr Oleander for what he is doing *now*."

"Ghosts don't," Alexis said. "They may be aware of things that have happened since their death, but it doesn't change their... their emotional register."

"Like Minnie Slocum," I said. "Still terrified of Zenobia Webster Tull."

"Yes, exactly." Alexis flashed me one of his brilliant, untrustworthy smiles. "Some are more focused than others, but they're all... they aren't people anymore. They're the memory of people. This thing was still a person, and it..."

"Was not, by any definition, sane."

Alexis opened his mouth to argue, then closed it again. "No. It's not sane."

"And if we don't know what it is," I said, "we have no hope of..." *Surviving the night* were the words on the tip of my tongue. "...Of banishing it."

"If that's even possible," Alexis said and seemed to collapse in on himself again. "Myra would know who it is."

"I'm sure Mrs Blackburn *does* know. And I suspect Mr Oleander could wager a guess."

"It knew *him*," Alexis agreed.

"It knew all of us, I think." I looked around the library in despair. We needed more information, and the books around us were spilling over with necromantic knowledge, but I did not think that even Zenobia Webster Tull's own writings would, in this case, give us the information we needed.

This was a house for keeping secrets, and we needed someone who would talk.

"Emily," I said.

"What?" Alexis jerked like I had offered him a galvanic shock.

"She's been here the longest, and she has no reason to keep T. Zacharias Tull's secrets for him. And I don't think... I don't think she's *quite* a ghost."

"She's only a little girl," Alexis said.

I stared at him. "We are not in a position to be, er, choosy."

"Mr Booth, do you really think—"

"Yes," I said flatly.

He would not do so aloud, but I could see in his face the desire to implore me to change my mind, to confess that I was joking. I was not joking. I had known that the house hated us for weeks; now, because we were a bunch of blind, stupid fools, we had drawn its attention to us. It could find us now, and although it might toy with us, I did not think it would toy for long.

Alexis dropped his gaze. "I can only work with a circle of seven or thirteen," he said.

"Then we need five," I said and stalked grimly to the door. "Come on. Let's find five while we still can."

I believe that Alexis followed me only because he did not want to be alone.

WE FOUND THE Order Aurorae Aeternae in the dining room. They had put the room back in order as best they could. No one seemed to have suggested going to bed, and I could see that, like Alexis, they were afraid to be alone. It was the first sign of common sense several of them had exhibited.

At least they did not need to be persuaded that there was a hostile spirit in the house. I made no attempt to interfere with Mrs Hallett's theorizing about the spirit's origin and purpose; I merely introduced the idea of another séance to search for information. Given the fierce jealousy that Mrs Blackburn had aroused in Mrs Hallett and Miss Quincey and Mrs Seftick, I suppose I should not have been surprised that none of them asked where she was. They *did* ask about Mr Oleander and Mr Kitchener, but I said truthfully that I had no more idea than they did.

No one suggested searching the grounds, which was a relief.

Mrs Hallett, Miss Parrington, Miss Quincey, and Mrs Seftick all agreed eagerly to another séance. Mr Seftick was hesitant; Mr Hallett (I thought) was drunk. Mr Bell looked carefully at Alexis and said, "Are you sure you should? You must already have expended a great deal of energy this evening."

Alexis looked surprised, whether at the mere idea or at the expression of concern I could not tell. He said, "I'm fine, thank you, Mr Bell, and I admit that I agree with Mr Booth that we should not wait."

Patterson Bell nodded. "Then let us—"

We heard a panicked shout: "*Oh dear God what—*" And then a scream.

The scream was guttural and shrill at once; it came from a human throat, but there was nothing human about it at all. It came from outside, north and east of the house. I do not know whether I knew that because of some clarity of the sound or only because I knew what it was.

Michael Kitchener. Dying horribly somewhere between the ornamental lake and the house.

The Order Aurorae Aeternae and Alexis and I ended up in a panicked clump by the fireplace. Mrs Seftick had her face buried in her husband's shoulder; his grip around her waist had to be hard enough to hurt. It was some moments before I was able to say, "We have to proceed."

Patterson Bell looked at me thoughtfully. "You know something."

"Not nearly enough," I said. "And Emily is the only person left to ask."

"All right," Mr Bell said. "Seftick, will you and Hallett watch the doors?"

It was a sensible suggestion, even if there was probably nothing they could do against either the thing out in the gardens or the spirit in the house. Mr Seftick nodded, and I was distantly aware of him arranging Mr Hallett in a chair by the north door while the seven of us settled around the table.

Alexis insisted on having me beside him. I had Mrs Hallett on my other side. Mr Bell sat to Alexis's right, then Miss Quincey, Mrs Seftick, and Miss Parrington, who was uncharacteristically silent, her eyes as round as an owl's.

This time Alexis did not indulge in any fancy histrionics. He gripped my hand and Mr Bell's hand tightly, leaned his head against the chair back, and said quietly, "We seek speech of Emily Tull. Emily, are you there?"

We waited. Without either Blackburn in the circle, Alexis seemed calmer, more patient. He murmured, "I know you're watching, Emily. I know you're frightened. You're trapped and you don't trust us. But we want to free you, you and the others who are trapped here. We need your help to do it. We need you to tell us what to do."

Slowly, I realized that I could feel her, too: a small, cold presence standing by the fireplace, just beyond the reach of my peripheral vision.

"You can talk to us, Emily," Alexis said. "Tell us what's trapped you here."

And finally, finally, a thin, faint voice said, "Why?"

"You're tired," Alexis said. "I know you want to rest."

"Why would you help me?" she asked suspiciously.

Alexis did not seem to know how to answer her, and Mrs Hallett took advantage of the pause to insert herself into the drama as it was her nature to do. "We *want* to help," she said. Before she could go on—for I suddenly knew that she was going to mention Mr Oleander—I said, "Tell us how to help you."

"It's the library man!" Emily said delightedly.

I tried not to flinch at being recognized and said again, "Tell us how to help you."

"Don't need help. It's too late."

A murmur of horror went around the table; Mrs Hallett's rings dug painfully into my hand. But Alexis interceded, perhaps recognizing as I had the necessity of keeping Mr Oleander's name from being spoken. "Why is it too late? Tell us."

"They've already killed us. It's too late."

"Who killed you?" Patterson Bell asked.

"No names," the voice said. "There aren't any names. Dead and gone."

"But you aren't gone," Alexis said. "You're trapped here. Your name is Emily."

There was no answer. She began to sing instead, "Bleu, Jaune, Vert," mispronouncing the words, and I could feel her wandering away.

"Wait!" Alexis said. "You don't have to talk about that. But at least tell us how he trapped you here. We *can* help with that."

"That wasn't *him*, silly," the voice said, and I thought it was the opportunity to correct his mistake that brought her back. "That's Mama's box."

"Mama's box?" Alexis said, rather faintly.

"The box with the house in it," said Emily.

"Oh God, it *is* in a book," I said barely hearing myself, remembering *The Dwelling of Souls* and my own idle speculation whether Zenobia Webster Tull had built her house to catch a genium loci.

"What box?" Alexis said. "Where?" But perhaps speaking to ghosts was something akin to holding a wet bar of soap. If one gripped too tightly, one lost the thing one tried to hold. Emily was gone.

IN THE AFTERMATH of the séance, I slipped away to check that the doors were bolted. I could no longer pretend not to understand the connection between Cecilia, who had died by drowning, and the thing that had pawed at the library doors, the thing that had almost certainly killed Michael Kitchener; I felt slightly better for the assurance that she was shut out.

When I returned, Alexis had managed to channel the Order's abundant energy in a potentially useful—or at least not actively harmful—direction.

"It will be like a giant treasure hunt," Miss Parrington said brightly.

I raised my eyebrows inquiringly.

"'Mama's box' seems to be the crux of the matter," Alexis said. "So I thought maybe we should try to find it."

"That seems, er, sensible," I said. "Just, er, nobody should go outside."

"Of course not," said Mrs Hallett. "Not while it's still dark. We shall search in pairs. Mr Booth, will you stay with Alexis? He needs to rest, and he said you intended to work in the library."

"Yes, er, of course."

"Splendid," said Mrs Hallett. She chivvied them out, assigning each pair a section of the house.

Alexis and I were carefully silent until her hectoring voice had died away, and then he gave a huge mock sigh of relief. "I had to do *something* to keep them busy."

"It's, er, a good idea. Though I don't expect... that is..."

"Oh, they're not going to *find* it. But it will keep them away from the library, and you said something about a book."

"...Yes."

"Well, then?" He gestured me out of the drawing room ahead of him.

"You, er, want to... that is, you don't mind if..."

"Please," Alexis said, and then looked as if he had surprised himself.

"Zenobia Webster Tull wrote a book," I said as we returned to the library, which was still mercifully silent and inviolate. "Actually, she wrote several, but there's one in particular..."

I slipped *The Dwelling of Souls* out from between its neighbors and brought it to the table. Alexis watched me, his face unreadable.

"It's a book about, er, the spirits of places, and she talks rather a lot... that is, she seems very interested in how you *make* a place have a spirit."

Alexis looked a little ill at the idea. "Can you?"

"Mrs Tull believed you could. And she gives very detailed instructions." I found the passage I wanted, and read it to Alexis: "A spirit may be bound to a specific place through the use of an object which partakes of the nature of both, though the object must be kept inviolate. Each living person who touches it will take away some small portion of the object's force with him, and eventually it will become ineffective, and the spirit will dissipate."

"So it's *very* well hidden," Alexis said.

"Yes. In the walls, rather than... Oh God," I said and sat down limply.

"Mr Booth?" Alexis said, sounding almost panicked.

"I… I've been having a dream. Recurrently." I told him about it as briefly as I decently could. "And I thought… in the dream I thought I was a man, but what if I wasn't? What if I was already dead and didn't know it?"

"You were a spirit," Alexis said.

"Walled in with Mrs Tull's box and whatever it contains."

"But I haven't felt anything remotely like that," Alexis objected after a moment. "Not in the séances, and not otherwise. That's not the presence I feel."

"No," I said. "I think, if I've, er, understood Mrs Tull's obfuscations properly, that the… that is, the trapped spirit is what generates the, er, presence you talk about. It isn't the presence itself. She *was* trying to create a genuine genium loci, to give the house a… a *consciousness* of its own, but she, er, chose a very dubious method."

"God. No wonder the house seems so hostile." He considered. "Myra would do something like that," he said, apparently to his hands. Then he clapped them together decisively and said, "All right. Where in the house would Mrs Tull have hidden her box?"

It was a dauntingly large question. I said, "There must be, er, plans of the house somewhere."

"Actually, there aren't. I remember because Myra wanted to see them, and Oleander said he'd never found any."

"How odd and unhelpful," I said. "Can you, er, dowse for it?"

"*Dowse* for it?"

"Can you feel it? Or the spirit trapped with it?"

"I don't know," Alexis said. "Maybe? I've never tried to do anything of the sort before. But I suppose I can't be any more useless than I am just sitting here. Shall we try?"

He stood up, giving me the loveliest smile of which I had ever been the recipient. "Let's," I said, and, pausing only to extinguish the lights, we left the library.

WE WANDERED THROUGH the main floor of the house without finding anything except the cold spot by the hatrack and the absolute destruction visited upon Zenobia Webster Tull's study. The study seemed like a logical—if obvious—place for anything belonging to Mrs Tull to be, and we spent some time picking through the wreckage before agreeing that there was nothing boxlike there.

We checked the Italianate staircase carefully for trapdoors or secret drawers, and found nothing.

On the second floor, we investigated Marcus Oleander's study first. It, too, had been visited by the cyclone, and I was more than ever grateful that the library had, for whatever reason, been spared. It was almost impossible to tell what sort of room Oleander's study had been, with all the drapes pulled down and the enormous desk flipped on its back like a helpless turtle, but everything was very dark—drapes, walls, furniture—and I thought Oleander had gone to some trouble to create the resemblance to a cave.

"It's all for show," Alexis said. "He never did any work in here."

I noticed the unthinking use of the past tense. "It doesn't look like... that is, there are no hiding places."

"If he'd had the box, we would have known. He would never have been able to resist bragging to Myra."

"I agree. The, er, question is whether there is a hiding place in here he wasn't aware of, and I don't think there was."

"Would you know how to tell if there was a secret niche behind the wainscotting?" he said mockingly.

I had no more patience for being mocked by Alexis Rigby. "No," I said and met his gaze steadily. "Would you?"

"No," he admitted after a moment, glancing at the ceiling. "And I do think, if it's the sort of thing we think it is, I'd be able to feel it, and I don't feel anything in here."

"Then let's move on," I said. "I, er, I don't think time is on our side."

"You think…"

"I think that the *genius* of this house may need time to, ah, regather itself after that tremendous burst of energy. But it certainly isn't *gone*."

"I take your point," Alexis said.

Knowing that Michael Kitchener was almost certainly lying dead in the gardens made searching his bedroom exceedingly unpleasant, especially as neither of us knew what we were looking for. I decided it made most sense to let Alexis act as a dowsing rod (or a coal miner's canary); therefore, I made much of figuring out the thickness of the walls while Alexis examined the furniture and the floor. I noticed that he looked at the ceiling twice before he said, "I don't think it's here."

"There's only Mr. Oleander's bedroom left," I said.

We shared a profoundly uneasy glance.

"We have to look," Alexis said. "Marcus told me that it was T. Zacharias's bedroom, and it must have been his mother's—so the box might really be there."

"Yes," I said, although I did not want to.

Marcus Oleander's bedroom, appointed in black and crimson, was exactly what I would have expected—except that the cyclone had been here, too, and the room was half-obscured by drifting feathers. The mirror was shattered in its frame; every drawer in the bureau had been pulled out and dumped on the floor. The closet doors were lolling open, and everything that should have been hanging in them had been pulled off its hangers. The bed, with all four posts leaning drunkenly together, looked like a collapsed black and crimson tent.

"Do you think," Alexis started to say when we heard Randolph fall down the stairs. It sounded even more horrifying from above; every ghastly sound seemed to echo. Even Alexis was rattled.

In the moment in which he was trying to regroup, he glanced at the ceiling again.

He said, "Do you really think it could be here?"

"I don't know," I said, "but I think we'd best at least look."

"Yes," he said unhappily.

We poked gingerly through the ruins of Marcus Oleander's bedroom and found nothing. When Alexis glanced at the ceiling again, I said, "Do you think it might be above us still?"

He frowned at me; I realized he hadn't been aware of his own movements and said apologetically, "You keep looking at the ceiling."

"Do I?" His frown deepened, but he directed it away from me to the stretch of plaster over our heads. "Yes," he said after a moment, and turned back to me. "A house like this must have attics, mustn't it?"

"T. Zacharias Tull died in the attic," I said, and Alexis and I stared at each other, wide-eyed with sudden certainty.

We left the bedroom gladly and, pausing only to find a flashlight, climbed the stairs to the third floor, which I knew, from something Oleander had said, had never been wired for electricity. I remembered and told Alexis, "This was the Cathcart nursery, where all the Cathcart children were killed."

He was playing the flashlight up and down the hall. He said, dismayed, "We're going to have to try all of these doors."

"Yes," I said, and I sounded just as dismayed as he did.

We looked at the doors nearest us. "One of these was the door to Louisa Cathcart's room."

"Do you know which side…?"

"I don't remember. Just that Louisa and Constance were on one side, and John Aloysius, Jr., and Rose on the other."

"Rose?" The light jerked.

"The oldest. She was telling you her name the whole time."

Alexis was silent for a moment, then said, "We have to start somewhere," and opened the door on the right.

Nothing. An empty little room that smelled strongly of dust. There were no other doors leading from this room, and Alexis closed the door on it with obvious relief.

He handed me the flashlight. My turn.

I opened the door on the left. Immediately, I heard a roaring noise, like lions at a great distance. I glanced at Alexis. He nodded, a short, sharp jerk of his chin. He heard it, too.

This room was as empty as the other one. I shut the door, and the roaring ceased—or at least I could no longer hear it.

We moved down the hall to the next pair of doors. Again, Alexis opened the door on the right. Again, we could both hear roaring, but the room was empty.

My side of the hall. I opened the door.

The next second I had slammed it shut, before what I saw had even fully registered on me.

"What?" Alexis said, barely above a whisper.

"Blood," I said. "That room is drenched in blood."

Alexis grimaced, the flashlight turning his face into a demon mask. "Was there another door?"

"I… I don't know."

"Then we have to look again. I think you're right about not having much time."

It sounded far less hypothetical when he said it. I pointed out to myself that it was not real blood and that, real or spectral, it could not harm me. I opened the door again.

There was nothing. The room was bare of furniture and innocent of blood, and there were no other doors. Only the roaring.

We moved onto the third set of doors. This time I went first and found an empty room.

Alexis opened the door on his side, and before he'd even turned the flashlight to illuminate the room, we both heard a heavy *thwack!* Alexis froze for a moment, then grimly turned the flashlight to examine the walls of the completely empty room. Another *thwack!* J. A. Cathcart dismembering his only son. There were no other doors. Alexis closed the door, and the noise stopped.

"All… all right," Alexis said. "There are only two doors left."

"Yes," I said and we moved down the hall to the last set of doors.

I opened the one on my side. Nothing, except that the roaring might have been slightly louder—and that might just as easily have been my imagination.

I shut the door, and Alexis and I shared an unhappy sidelong look. Alexis said, "If it isn't behind this door, I don't know what we'll do."

"Check the ceiling," I said. We both looked up, and Alexis shone the flashlight into every corner, but there was no trapdoor.

"We have to," Alexis said.

"We do," I said, "although I am afraid to."

He laughed, not in mockery, but in surprised recognition. "I am, too."

We were silent for a long moment before he said again, "We have to."

"Yes," I said and came around him to face the last door.

"All right," he said and opened the door.

The room was empty.

Alexis shone the flashlight carefully around the walls, and there *was* another door in the back left corner.

"That must be it," Alexis said. He started across the room, but jerked to a halt when it suddenly became apparent that the room was not empty after all.

She was translucent, a girl of thirteen or fourteen, standing in the middle of the room with her hands stretched out to us imploringly. Her nightgown was soaked in blood, and there was a great, gaping hole in the middle of her chest. After a moment of terror so acute it was physically painful, I realized that she was not moving.

"Rose," I said, although my voice wobbled and skied. "Her father hacked her heart out of her chest, and I wish I had it to give back to her."

"God," said Alexis. He had retreated to stand beside me again. "What do we do? Do we just walk around her?"

"What else *can* we do?" I said, to which he had no answer.

We skirted wide around Rose Cathcart, almost clinging to the walls. Although she seemed to be facing me every time I gave into the compulsion to look at her, she did not move, and we reached the door without further surprises.

"Watch it be locked," Alexis said as he tried the knob, but it opened with only the shriek of the hinges to suggest how long it had been since anyone went up to the attic of Thirdhop Scarp. The stairs were steep and narrow, and mercifully they led up.

Alexis started up and I followed. It was apparent almost immediately that we were finally on the right track, because Alexis staggered and said, "I can feel it. It doesn't want us up here. And it doesn't want… It *is* the house, it's the house and all the people who died here, and—blessed mother of God, what is that horrible wet thing on the terrace?"

"Ah," I said, and because suddenly there seemed no choice at all, I shoved him ahead of me up the steps. "That would be Cecilia."

"Cecilia?" Alexis said, almost too shrill to be audible, and of course he didn't know about the fates of Zenobia Webster Tull's children. He had never given me the chance to tell him. As we came into the attic proper, I saw that it must be nearly dawn, hard though that was even to imagine. But light was beginning to seep in through the louvers.

"She drowned in the ornamental lake," I said. "And I think T. Zacharias—"

"He killed her," Alexis said; the flashlight was enough to show his face too pale, and his eyes wide and blank. "Not with his hands, not like he did Emily, but he got her out in the lake and he wouldn't let her get out and he held her under and under, and oh sweet Christ, she's found a way in."

"I must have missed a door," I said, feeling guilt and panic like a stitch in my side. "Alexis. Alexis!"

I shook him, and finally he blinked, and his eyes focused on me. He said, "She's going to be heading for us. To stop us. We have to find the box."

"She can't climb stairs," I said.

"Want to bet?" he said harshly. "The house is calling her. Like a dog-whistle to a dog. I don't think stairs are going to stop her."

Whether he was right or wrong, we were really down to only the one option. "We have to find the box."

"And we know it must be up here," Alexis said, "or why would the house be in such a panic?" He swung the flashlight around, and we both groaned at the masses of furniture, boxes, steamer trunks that loomed on every side.

"I'm going to close the door," I said. "Lock it, if I can."

"Yes. Please."

"It's *inside* the house," I said. "We know that. Don't bother with the outside walls." I flung myself back down the attic stairs, slammed the door shut. There was a keyhole, but where the key might be... dear God in Heaven, was there ever such a futile question? I caromed back up to the attic, grabbed the nearest broken-backed chair, and wrestled it down, wedging it under the doorknob, across the doorframe. I did not delude myself for a second that it would stop her, but it might impede her. At least it would give us warning.

Back to the attic, and I followed the flashlight's radiance to Alexis, who was clawing his way through a collection of long abandoned winter coats. "It feels...

different… over here," he panted as he heard me behind him. I joined him in shoving the bulky coats aside, biting my lip against a curse as Emily's plaintive voice began singing "Bleu, Jaune, Vert," somewhere in the dust and darkness behind us.

"It's the house," Alexis said under his breath, almost chanting. "It's the *house*."

"What's the house?" I said—anything to distract myself from the child's pathetic French. There were boxes stacked behind the coats; we began throwing them, heedless of their contents, anything to get to the wall.

"It kills people," Alexis said. "There's blood in the foundations, I don't know whose. And Zacharias killed his sister when he was thirteen. He killed all his sisters, and his mother, and the house helped. He didn't kill his brother, though, or his father. The house…" A horrified, jerky giggle. "The house did those on its own."

Randolph Tull, I remembered, had fallen down the stairs, dead drunk, at the age of thirty-three. Leonard Tull had died of a heart attack in one of the unused bedrooms and was not found for nearly ten hours.

"And it killed *him,* too. When he was old and wasn't strong enough and got frightened and tried to find the box. It killed him so it could keep him."

I scraped my knuckles bloody against plaster, and we heard, very plain over Emily's singing, the clatter of something trying to open the door at the bottom of the stairs.

"It's *here*," Alexis said. "I can feel it now. Cold and dark and hard, and dear God, so dead. So very dead."

I looked around wildly; there was an antlered hatstand like a demented tree leaning against a steamer trunk. I grabbed it and drove it desperately against the wall, my attention straining backwards, downwards, to the attic door, and the patient, fumbling crashes and clatters of Cecilia slowly destroying my impromptu barricade.

With a crunch, the iron-shod foot of the hatstand sank into the wall; I wrenched it free and struck again harder, my breath coming in short, painful screams of effort, again, again—and then Alexis said, "There! I can reach! Wait, wait!" I waited, nearly off balance with the weight of the hatstand, and Alexis leaned forward, scrabbling in plaster and lath.

I heard, very clearly, the chair give way.

"Got it!" Alexis shouted. He jerked back, hands bleeding, holding a long rectangular box. I dropped the hatstand and went to my knees, helping him with the catches, which were stiff with rust. Emily's song was getting louder—was she trying to mask Cecilia's approach, or warn us of it?—and I could hear Cecilia sighing and snuffling her way up the stairs.

Alexis swore viciously as a catch pinched his fingers, and then, together, we threw the lid back, revealing a fat roll of…

"Architect's drawings," I said blankly.

Phythias Ormont's plans of Thirdhop Scarp, and I knew whose spirit Zenobia Webster Tull had trapped here to make her genium loci.

The flat stagnant stench I remembered was suddenly pervasive; I did the only thing I could think of. I grabbed the plans and began tearing them in half.

Emily screamed, a high, wailing, painful sound. Cecilia was screaming, too, bellowing, and I would not turn around, *did* not turn around, not until the plans of Thirdhop Scarp were confetti around us, and by then there was nothing there to see.

Nothing there at all.

I knelt there, one hand anchored in the hatstand's rack of antlers, the other braced against the dusty boards of the floor, my chest heaving as I coughed rackingly against the plaster dust and cobwebs. It was some time before I could catch my breath again, and when I did, when I could hear over the thunder of my own blood in my ears, I realized there was another noise, something moaning. I picked up the flashlight and looked around carefully.

The barest flash of movement from the corner farthest from the door. The moaning, like a dog in terrible pain, was coming from Alexis Rigby.

VI

Marcus Oleander was found at the bottom of Thirdhop Scarp with his neck and most of the other bones in his body broken. The police decided there were no signs of foul play, and discovered furthermore that Mr Oleander's finances were in such bad condition as to be called bankrupt. It was ruled death by misadventure, but the story that started going around almost immediately was that he'd jumped rather than face his flock when they learned what had happened to their money.

It was certainly better than the truth.

Marcus Oleander died intestate, for if he had had a will, it had been one of the things destroyed in Zenobia Webster Tull's parlor. The house at Thirdhop Scarp and everything in it were put up for auction, and Christabel Hallett, granddaughter of Zenobia Webster Tull, planted front and center with her husband at her side, bid grimly and fiercely, and bought the entire estate. "My birthright," she told newspapers, and immediately began reforming, in both senses of the word, the Order Aurorae

Sarah Monette

Aeternae. Since she had all the sensitivity to the occult of a Chippendale sideboard, it seemed unlikely she could do any harm, even in that house. Miss Quincey and Mrs Seftick became her chief disciples. I do not think Mrs Hallett will make the mistakes Mr Oleander did.

Michael Kitchener was discovered drowned in the ornamental lake.

Miss Parrington, museum gossip says, is in California, learning about her past lives.

I have not heard that anyone ever saw Myra Blackburn or her husband again. Wherever she is and whatever she is calling herself now, the past will find her eventually. It always does.

Once a month, I take the train to a small, slumberous town called Blakely, where I hire the only taxi-cab to drive me to Blanchard House. It is a private sanitarium, well-funded, discreet, and with far higher standards for its staff than any state asylum could ever aspire to.

I do not believe that Alexis recognizes me. I visit because *someone* must and because as far as I know Alexis has no one else.

His given name, it turned out, was Jonathan Lesley; he grew up in Hestonville, a small town in upper New York State. I can find nothing about his family except that his father was a "learned man and had suffered many disappointments." When Jonathan was eleven, he was placed in the care of a family named Falconer. When he was thirteen, the family's own son, Matthew Falconer, then aged nine, was found in one of the mausoleums in the Hestonville cemetery; he had been burned to death. Matthew, I learned, had been a fey, dreamy child. There had been a game he played with his friends, about which none of them would provide more than the barest of fragments, that had involved talking to "imaginary friends." A game that had always been played in the cemetery, and it was not hard to guess why.

I was told that Jonathan Lesley inherited a small number of books from his father; almost certainly, Conrad Oettinger was among them.

When Jonathan was fourteen, he was caught accepting money to act as a medium. The Falconers, assuming he was a fraud, were horrified that he would take advantage of people's grief in that fashion and forbade him to continue. He ran away; no one in Hestonville ever heard from him again. How he became entangled with the Blackburns, when and why he changed his name: those are questions to which I will probably never have answers. Not until the day Alexis can tell me himself, if that day ever comes.

I did find a photograph—perhaps the only surviving photograph of Jonathan Lesley and Matthew Falconer—and just as I visit Alexis once a month in Blanchard House, so I have the photograph hanging on my wall: two boys in dark suits and stiff collars, their hair slicked back severely against their skulls. The elder has his arm around the younger boy's shoulders, and it is probably only hindsight that makes me see possessiveness in the way his white hand lies against the dark cloth.

ACKNOWLEDGMENTS

THANKS GO TO Ambar, Sabine Moehler, Paige Morgan, Linda Martinez, Sharis Ingram, Hilary Kraus, Laura E. Price, Jeff Frane, Garret Reece, Oliver Barrett, Mariam Kvitsiani, Jesper Stage, Katie Jones, E.S.H., Cindy Deichmann, Lynne Everett, Laura Bailey, Gabe V, Ruthanna and Sarah Emrys, Lesley Hall, Sarah Ervine, M&M Reppy, Jennifer G Tifft, Cecil I. Roth, Teresa Doyle Kovich, Ruby "wizardcake" Jeffrey, Sasha Lydon, Lindsay Kleinman, Katherine Magruder, and all my other Patreon patrons.

Thanks *also* go to the friends who keep me sane: Elizabeth Bear, Arkady Martine, John Chu, Fade Manley, Max Gladstone, Celia Marsh, C. L. Polk, Jodi Meadows, Amal El-Mohtar, Ryan Van Loan, Benjamin C. Kinney, Alex Haist, Devin Singer, Liz Bourke, Fran Wilde, Amanda Downun, Scott Lynch, Jamie Rosen, Clarissa C. S. Ryan, John Wiswell, Sarah Terentiev.

Thanks to my agent, Cameron McClure. Thanks to Amanda Rutter and everyone at Solaris.

And especial thanks to my husband, Allen Monette, who has read *A Theory of Haunting* more times than either of us can count.

ABOUT THE AUTHOR

Sarah Monette and Katherine Addison are the same person.

She was born in Oak Ridge, Tennessee, one of the three secret cities of the Manhattan Project. She got her B.A. from Case Western Reserve University, her M.A. and Ph.D. from the University of Wisconsin-Madison. Despite being *summa cum laude*, none of her degrees is of the slightest use to her in either her day job or her writing, which she feels is an object lesson for us all.

She has published more than fifty short stories, seven solo novels, and three collaborations with her friend Elizabeth Bear. *The Goblin Emperor* won the 2015 Locus Award for Best Fantasy Novel and was a finalist for the Hugo, the Nebula, and the World Fantasy Award. *The Angel of the Crows* was nominated for the 2021 Locus Award.

She lives, with spouse, cats, and books, somewhere near Madison, Wisconsin.

FIND US ONLINE!

www.rebellionpublishing.com

/solarisbooks   /solarisbks   /solarisbooks

SIGN UP TO OUR NEWSLETTER!

rebellionpublishing.com/newsletter

YOUR REVIEWS MATTER!

Enjoy this book? Got something to say?

Leave a review on Amazon, Goodreads or with your
favourite bookseller and let the world know!

THESE LIFELESS THINGS

PREMEE MOHAMED

"GASP-OUT-LOUD ASTONISHING"
– CHARLIE JANE ANDERS ON *BENEATH THE RISING*

SATELLITES

SOLARISBOOKS.COM

POLLEN FROM A
FUTURE HARVEST

DEREK KÜNSKEN

"KÜNSKEN'S VIVID WORLDBUILDING IS A
KNOCKOUT" – *PUBLISHERS WEEKLY*

SATELLITES

SOLARISBOOKS.COM

THE DIFFICULT LOVES
OF MARIA MAKILING

WAYNE SANTOS

SATELLITES

SOLARISBOOKS.COM

KID WOLF AND KRAKEN BOY

SAM J. MILLER

SATELLITES

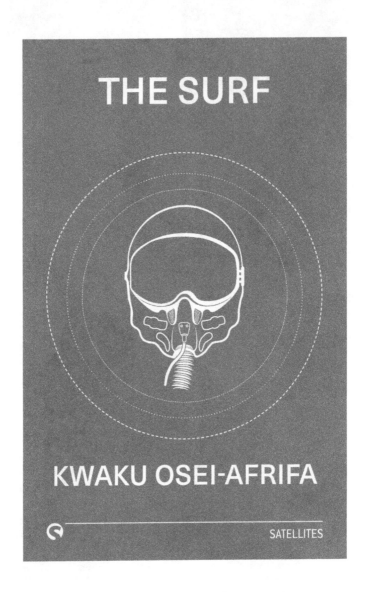

THE SURF

KWAKU OSEI-AFRIFA

SATELLITES

◌ SOLARISBOOKS.COM

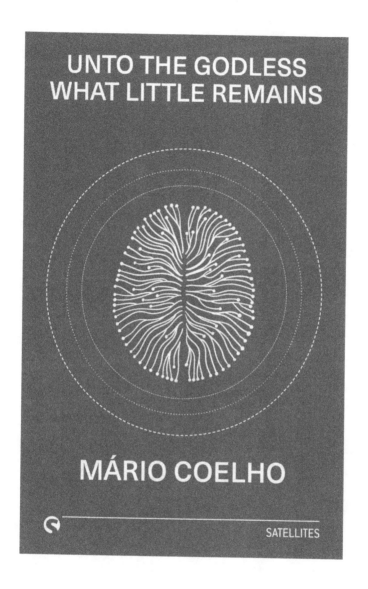

UNTO THE GODLESS
WHAT LITTLE REMAINS

MÁRIO COELHO

SATELLITES

SOLARISBOOKS.COM

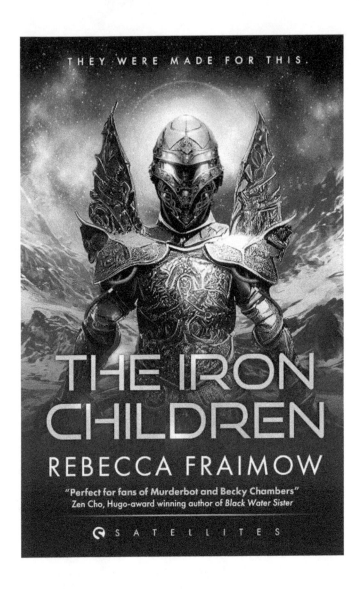

THEY WERE MADE FOR THIS.

THE IRON CHILDREN

REBECCA FRAIMOW

"Perfect for fans of Murderbot and Becky Chambers"
Zen Cho, Hugo-award winning author of *Black Water Sister*

SATELLITES

⊙ SOLARISBOOKS.COM

Printed in the USA
CPSIA information can be obtained
at www.ICGtesting.com
BVHW031310220823
668788BV00002B/131

9 781837 861101